I0678404

Praise for The Boy and the Islands:

"Everything takes place in a dilated, fleeting time. A layered novel, where space/time overlapping seems to determine the fate of the characters, always in search of their freedom: a young boy, a future writer who, on the one hand, flees from an apprehensive mother and, on the other, pursues the destiny that a ball draws before him, going beyond the railroad tracks without crossing them. As the author points out in his note, this book is 'a map, something purely geographical and at the same time chronological'."

—Adrián N. Bravi, *Doppiozero*

"Magliani's book is populated by characters who, meeting by chance between the present and the past, exchange a few words, share breakfast or dinner, become curious about each other, and exercise rustic and informal hospitality with an ancient, natural grace. We have already encountered this affability in Magliani's works: those who welcome others want nothing in return, just a little company, a chat that broadens the horizon a little; and those who wander (because people often wander in Magliani's work, and if there are those who welcome, there are those who wander, and vice versa, it is human nature, and also in the sense of Magliani's writing, I believe), those who wander are grateful to take a break, to find shelter, not to be looked at askance or sent away rudely."

—Claudio Morandini, *Diacritica*

"We can say that *The Boy and the Islands (A Dream of Calvino's)*, a dreamy, inspiring, evocative, and poignant novel, is a tribute to Calvino and to literature in general, in which Marino Magliani now rightfully occupies a prominent place."

—Francesco Improta, *RPlibri*

Voci italiane 1

Marino Magliani

THE BOY AND THE ISLANDS
(A DREAM OF CALVINO'S)

Translated by Orianna Soublette

CASA LAGO PRESS

Voci italiane
Volume 1

This series is dedicated to those works directly related to Italy, which may have their origins in Italy or abroad. They may be prose, poetry, criticism, history, and the like.

This book was translated thanks to a grant awarded by the Italian Ministry of Foreign Affairs and International Cooperation.

COVER IMAGE: "Punta Falconara," a watercolor by Lino Pastorelli used here with the kind permission of the painter.

ISBN 978-1-955995-16-0
Library of Congress Control Number: Available upon request.

© 2025 Marino Magliani

All rights reserved.
Printed in the United States of America

CASA LAGO PRESS
New Fairfield, CT

TABLE OF CONTENTS

PUBLISHER'S NOTE

We are most grateful to Marino Magliani for his confidence in entrusting his book to Casa Lago Press. For us it is a privilege and an honor, and as such, we wanted to have it inaugurate a new series, *Voci italiane*.

Of course, our heartfelt thanks go out to Orianna Soublette who took on this translation with great enthusiasm. In addition to Orianna we also thank Stephen Cerulli for his diligent proof reading.

Dulcis in fundo, Emanuele Pettener brought this book to us, one of his numerous activities behind much of what we do here at Casa Lago Press, especially in Italian.

Sanremo, Summer 1935

Awaiting the end of the tunnel, the game was in counting to twenty and yet, inevitably, arriving a bit late or early. Sort of like for that frontier, contorted and frequented by his people, the consciousness of being in the right place and still having time to escape. Was that why he was returning to Sanremo, to be close to Menton? Or was he only returning because he was out of money?

But since the tracks had flanked the sea, he had hardly thought about the play of light and the frontiers that awaited him. As he closed his eyes, other cliffs resurfaced, much whiter and more porous, perhaps only more African. And now and then, as he raised his eyelids, he could recognize in the colors and volumes the precise memory of that other trip to the Ligurian coast. Did it not belong, after all, to the same Mediterranean story, through the routes of a private archipelago that was drawn during all those years?

Then, notebook open on his lap and pencil ready on the seat—as had happened to him some time before during a car ride in Ibiza—once he reached Alassio, with its green island in front of it, he began to draw it, and to extend the sea to Cape Mele, as if that expanse now too formed an island in front of the island. And below the vignette, he repeated the exercise of the waves:

In front of the sea, obstacles aside, they say
it does it all.

He would share the meaning of it with the rest of the passengers, in his own language, or in French, which he spoke well. *Tiens, tiens.* If one thinks of the sea, one may also think of nothing. It does it all.

The passengers saw him smiling as the train expelled itself from the mountain. Absorbed by the glass for some time, bouncing across the surface of the sea, the light penetrated the carriage. Through the upper window, opened a palm's width, an irritable wisp of dust slipped in, and the odorous cold of the tunnels forced his eyes closed. And when he opened them again, neither he nor the sea smiled as before.

The air shivered, as if it were the sea itself asking it to do so each evening, and the air obeyed. The waves rolled in nervously, then suddenly became calm, spilling over the rocks as if from inertia, over the few fistfuls of earth and brushwood from which sprouted rows of agave and a trail of sea foam, which hardly waited for the next wave's sea foam before returning to the sea. Toward the rest of the parched landscape, at the top of the escarpment and up to the edges of the gravel and crossties, came only the promise of salty vapors.

On the side of the train facing the mountain, he went to see why the train had stopped. Even the rusted stone walls and fig trees were those of a season and sunset he knew well. A mineral deposit crumbled from the sky, the beginning of the collapse, amid solid terraces, the laborers bent over the earth.

Last night, he had watched the moon for a long time, sitting on the edge of the little wall in the garden below the inn. The beaches burned brightly, until the sun was extinguished, just before dawn. Then, Corsica had seemed different to him every day. And one evening, returning from the fields above Sanremo, he saw the great cemetery full of the death of his people.

When the train started screeching again in waves, to stop shortly after and fall silent, a brood of cicadas rose from the plants and assailed the silence.

He waited on the platform for the passengers to disperse, and then for the workers to unload their luggage. A breeze faintly inflated the station tarps, stirring only the fronds of a palm tree for a few moments. Suddenly, however, the wind grew stronger, as if a second train had passed, and people looked up at the sky.

What was this terraced Liguria, with its rocky sky that unleashed without warning, promised rains, and soon subsided? The place of frontiers, this he knew; the shelter, here and there, to take before continuing on to other mountains, to Brigasque territory, beyond the olive valleys, to the north, or to the south, to the ports of Marseilles, from which one might reach its islands.

The seagulls ducked uncertainly in midair, quieter than insects, then grew tired and took to the now dull ruts of the creek, with its houses on the bank. But even down there, it was as if they returned from a deserted meadow.

Verde. Villa Verde. He had said its name a couple of times, and the bellhop had furrowed his brow because this was not a place where tips were given. The man picked up the suitcases, placed them on the cart, and he followed. The screeching of wheels came from the cars in the square, and only then did he see that the two people sitting on the bench under the palm trees were children. He noticed their nice clothes and that they were of an age which indicated they were still children, but would likely not be by the end of summer.

Suffocated by the heat again, despite it already being evening, he listened to the people, remembering their chant of glowing words after so long.

He looked halfway up the hillside, at a point in the terraces to the east of Villa Verde, for the farmer who toiled in the vegetable gardens up there. He had that habit of spitting on his hands before grabbing the garden hoe. Every now and then, he would stand up straight, wipe his forehead with the back of his hand, and look at the roofs of Villa Verde and the Astoria Hotel. Then he would twirl the knotted handkerchief around his neck, wasting time, and he liked to justify that suffocating heat: *messieur*, in the winter, we pray for this.

A place where the heat was not mentioned, but rather accepted, one put up with a little bit of everything in the fields above Sanremo and in the end, one makes do with little, Dora had explained to him, the rest was for the rich and tourists.

"Are you Russian?" one of the children said in French. Removing his feet from his sandals, he had lifted his legs onto the bench, hugging them and resting his chin on his knees.

He had stood near the car, waiting for the bellhop to put the things in the trunk.

"German. My name is Walter," he replied in French.

"I'm Duilio, this is Italo."

Italo kept silent, sitting like Duilio and not seeming to suffer from the heat.

"Isn't that suitcase heavy?" asked Duilio.

It was a leather suitcase, sleek, with somewhat frustrated corners, and indeed, it was strange that Walter had not handed it to the bellhop with the rest.

"*Stentuassu*," said a man of toil. That's it, he recalled, that's what those people called this suffocating heat.

"*Tiens, tiens*, a suitcase full of children's books carries weight. Aren't you going to dinner?"

Italo blinked and raised his eyes to the palm fronds, the air moving the long glossy leaves, barely lifting them.

Duilio replied, "The church bells haven't rang yet."

Maybe you can look for it again, he thought as he arranged his things in the room. Last time, he had waited for it for a long time, hiding in a karst wrinkle among the gorse, but it had not passed by. The farmer spitting in his hands had warned him, "It's clever, it notices if someone is around."

From the balcony of Villa Verde, he heard the chimes of the *Hail Mary*. The laborers halted and gathered their tools, returning from their terraces, the mules in line. At this hour, the two little boys should have been on their way home, too. One, the taciturn and observant one, was named Italo; the other's name, he could not remember. Yet he was the one who had talked the most.

Yes, maybe you'll see it. It used to reproduce up there, away from the Riviera, where people escaping pass through. He had read that it was the largest saurian in Europe and lived only in Liguria, the Pyrenees, and the Balearic Islands, but he had never seen it in Ibiza.

From the window facing the mountain, the cool air glued a new light to the leaves. Perhaps it had rained. By the seaside rose the daylight, dragging with it an already tired buzz of bathers and carriages.

Walter went to Dora's house and a blond woman appeared in the doorway.

He pointed out to her the presence of a child outside the gate. "He was at the station last night. When I got off the train, he must have heard that I was coming here...."

"And he followed you? Here they don't follow tourists like in Naples."

Walter looked at a spot on the window frame. *I'd like to be a tourist*, he thought. *To have the privilege, and not be here because you have no money or think of nothing but frontiers.*

He wore a dress shirt over his undershirt and filled the pipe, some smoke came out. He moved the papers on the table and placed one of the children's books from the suitcase on it.

Dora smiled. "I wasn't going to read it." She was referring to the letter that lay on the table and was now covered.

Walter paused in the doorway, as if to comment, then smiled, too, and continued down the stairs.

Italo had his back to him, pretending not to notice him and then almost not to recognize him.

Walter joined him.

"I need a helper, do you know the names of the fields and towns and plants?"

"From a to z, my father is a botanist who studies plants and designs framework for flowers. Up here, he tells me, someday it will all be windows lined with flowers." He had not said greenhouses. He seemed quite happy to make small talk, but the names of the plants interested him less, and perhaps with someone who walked around with such luggage, one could discuss much more.

"You speak French well, too."

Italo bent his head to one side.

"Duilio doesn't believe the suitcase is full of children's books."

"Do you?"

"I do. Are they in French?"

"German. Do you want to hear some of the titles? There are also a couple in French."

"Then one in German and one in French."

"*Die Welt in Bildern.* The one in French is: *Choix de contes. Pour la jeunesse.* They are illustrated books. Illustrations are important."

Italo nodded. He agreed—no doubt about it—of course they were.

They both looked up at the window because Dora had appeared. Before saying something in German and retreating again, she smiled.

Walter had answered her.

"Is that your wife?" asked Italo, waiting until they had finished talking.

"She was."

"Do you draw?"

"With Dora?"

"No, do you—"

"Sure, I mean, I write a story about a man who draws islands, and in order for him to draw them, I have to teach myself first. Don't you think?"

"I think so. Do you only draw islands or also the sea?"

"Also the sea; if you draw an island, you have to draw the sea, too."

Italo nodded. They looked for it, among the branches, and said nothing. From that garden, maybe they could talk more about the palm trees and ficus and less about the sea. They could talk about things, those between the eyes and the first wave, but about what lay beyond, Walter said, what was there to say? Italo thought about it and this time, he did not nod. Walter gave him a few moments to comment. Since Italo was taking too long, Walter repeated the words written in the notebook.

The sea does it all. *Tiens, tiens*, the sea does it all. Italo hid his lips.

"So you know the trails and fields above Sanremo."

Italo moved his hand from side to side. "Yes, one by one, all the way to the Armea Valley. We have several of them too; the most beautiful is the one in San Giovanni."

"I was in San Giovanni last year, and I never met you...maybe you've already seen the ocellated lizard."

"Do you know it? My father found a skeleton of one, a beast like this." He spread his arms out a little.

"You're exaggerating."

"I swear. So you know it...."

"Let's just say I look for it."

"It never shows itself."

"I'm afraid not."

Before evening, Italo went out. He was looking forward to being able to go to the movie theater with his friends, but for now, he had to make do with the steps from which to watch the boys play soccer. The squares rested at an incline, and most of their time was spent chasing the ball before it went down the alleys. The old men sitting in front of the houses threatened to puncture it.

He and Duilio had gone up to Our Lady of the Coast, above the houses, sitting against the stump of an olive tree and keeping their eyes on the wispy expanse of roofs and balconies collapsing toward the Via Aurelia.

"He gave me the names of some of the titles. My father told me that he is Jewish, and that Villa Verde is full of Jews. Do you know what he's looking for?"

"What do I know."

"The ocellated lizard. Don't tell anyone."

They had not set a time to meet, but Italo had tried to guess and, having gone down to the Via Aurelia, seeing all those people in the sea, it seemed to him to be the right time.

Indeed, Villa Verde's guests would go outside and get lost in the tree-lined streets, toward Corso Imperatrice and the beaches.

Walter caught sight of him beyond the gate and put down his pen, stood up, and put on his dress shirt.

They looked at the plants as one looks at the sea, hands behind their backs, slightly bent forward, and head tilted to one side. They looked like a father and son who say almost nothing to each other and occasionally cross their arms. And when they sat down on the bench, they both crossed their legs.

"So you went out with your friend last night?"

"I was watching them play soccer from Our Lady of the Coast when Duilio asked me why you're looking for the ocellated lizard."

"Because in life you have to look for something. Tell him the important thing is not to find it, otherwise you have nothing more to look for, and you must look for it, otherwise it will look for you. As for the lizard, it is extremely beautiful, don't you think? I have seen drawings of it; it is bright green with blue circles on its back." He made a gesture not knowing quite how to say eyespots in French. "In early summer, it finishes mating and during the winter, it hides in the cracks. But your father must know these things well."

Italo did not entirely understand and changed the subject.

"Don't you ever go to the sea? People come here for the sea."

"I stay inside, I watch it; that's enough for now. And I draw, I study saurians. Do you go to the sea often?"

"We swim by the shipwreck, then go up to play soccer, but the ball always rolls downhill." He wanted to say the alleys, but didn't know how to say it in French.

"Then when you're tired and go home, you should draw and write, too. The story of the ball rolling away and getting lost in alleys is beautiful."

"There is nothing special about a ball hitching a ride," he said half in Italian and half in dialect.

"There's nothing special in the world if you don't make it special. What's at the bottom of the hills?"

"The tracks, a bunch of tracks pass through."

"Then write about the ball's path and at the bottom of the hill, make it end up at the tracks."

"It can't reach them, there's a railing."

"I have never seen the ocellated lizard in the flesh or even in bones, just as I don't know any man who draws islands, but I wrote about him, and now there are islands and there is a man who draws islands. Balls may very well bounce over the railings, *tiens, tiens.*"

"Then I'll write that the ball passes through there and the child leaves it there because his mother said you don't cross the tracks...."

"What if he wants the ball back at all costs?"

Italo breathed deeply, pursed his lips, and all that oxygen formulated a partial solution.

"He could go as far as where the tracks end without crossing them and, once he's there, go back and get the ball—"

"Too complicated. At that point, he has to grab the ball and go back to where the tracks end to go around all over again. Do you understand?"

Italo certainly understood; things were exactly as Mr. Walter said.

In the meantime, the bells tolled the *Hail Mary*, and Italo said he had to go home in two minutes. Walter asked him where he lived. Italo pointed upward. One had to walk all the way up the trail, past the benches at the station where they sat with Duilio, cross the Via Aurelia, then behind the Hotel Paris and the casino, and climb back up part of the Pigna. His house was above, not right on the San Giovanni road, but almost.

Walter said it was like going to where the tracks end, so he had to hurry if he wanted to get there in time for dinner.

He saw him pass through the gate at a good pace and disappear shortly after. He stayed outside a little longer looking at the windows of the inn; he had no desire to return inside that evening, although his room was now getting cooler. He had received a letter from Adorno in the morning, and he could have answered him and told him that he had not yet seen the lizard.

Italo dodged the muleteers and bicycles, threading his way through the tourists in front of the ice cream parlor. He was already fantasizing about their next meeting; maybe they would look at books together, it was Mr. Walter who had told him he wanted to bring the whole suitcase down sometime. Italo had gladly agreed, without imagining that his father would recruit him and his brother to go up to the fields in San Giovanni to pick green beans for a few days.

One evening, having returned well before dinner from work in the fields, he presented himself under the windows of Villa Verde. Walter came down with only one booklet.

Italo read the title (it was in French), flipped through it, and looked at the back cover. He did not mention that he was expecting to see the whole suitcase, but at the same time, could not hide his disappointment. Walter noticed this and made up an excuse; he didn't want to tell him that carrying the whole suitcase and opening it on the benches might attract attention, and then spending time with a young boy.... People passed by at every moment, the mansion was being watched.

Italo returned the booklet.

"In return, I'd like to take you to look for the ocellated lizard. I told a muleteer about it, the father of a friend of mine. There are several places where we can see it, with any luck."

"*Tiens, tiens*...thank you, but it wouldn't be good, you know, for them to see us out together in the countryside. These are not good times."

Italo frowned.

They met four more times. Walter was not always in his room, but when he was, upon seeing Italo, he tapped his knuckles in the glass to tell him he was coming down. The last time, along with a book, he brought a banana from France.

Italo ate it and said, "My father used to grow them. There are a lot of them in Cuba."

"And you've been to Cuba?"

"I was born there, I already told you."

In fact, he had already explained it to him, and for the second time, at that strange declaration of birth, Walter had smiled.

"But are you sure?"

"*Belin*, do you want me to not know where I was born?" he said seriously, half in Italian.

"Cuba must be beautiful, I would like to go there soon. To the Cubans I would say, 'Ladies and gentlemen, Italo, Cuban-born story-teller of alleys and terraces, sends his regards from Sanremo.'"

"Born in Santiago de las Vegas, Republic of Cuba, in the Caribbean Sea."

Not on the night of the banana, but a few days later, Walter, half-amused, said that he might as well leave at this point. They had not found the ocellated lizard, but he had shown him the books and even translated the titles.

He thought he would be a little sorry, but Italo tilted his head and only wanted to know what day and time he was leaving.

On June 22, year XIII of the fascist era, or 1935, Walter had to catch the train before the evening and Italo met him at the station.

When the carriage arrived from underneath Corso Imperatrice, Duilio was also waiting on the platform. They stood under the palm tree, and Duilio told Italo to ask him why the leather suitcase was not among his luggage. Italo would have asked him even if Duilio had not pointed it out.

Walter joked about it. "*Tiens, tiens,* the suitcase of books...." And he spread his arms wide. "I knew I was forgetting something...." Then he told them the truth. He had left it on purpose in Sanremo, so that next year they would look at the books together again. Under better conditions, more calmly.

Italo knew that Walter would return to Liguria. They had already agreed Walter would write to Dora, who would let him know whenever Italo came by Villa Verde.

By the time the train arrived, the *Hail Mary* had long since sounded, and Italo and Duilio had to say goodbye to Walter.

Once alone, Walter had felt a kind of melancholy, the same kind as when he thought of places like Cuba, or boarded a train, and he was agitated by the strange feeling to return somewhere and stop, sooner or later, during the trip.

The mountains, above the terraces of olive trees, shone a rough blue. Soon, night would fall and a trace of that blue would remain, like the sloughed skin of reptiles among the cliffs.

THE TRACKS

It is a winter afternoon, the sun is in a hurry. A child says to his mother, "I'm going down to play soccer."

"Don't sweat."

The child disobeys and Gino, who has been the goalie a lot today and has to retrieve the ball every time, also sweats. Strange rule, whoever blocks the penalty kick then goes to kick, taking the run-up from the bottom of the square.

Shadows slowly bite into the stones and plaster of one side of the alley. A goal without posts, the corner and two steps that meet at a shaky front door make up the goal line. For the crossbar, if the ball hits under Mrs. Angiolina's shutter, who always keeps it closed at a certain time in the afternoon because of the soccer balls, it is a goal. Two out of three times, the ball goes through the porch and past the corner, bounces, goes downhill, and depending on how steep it is, rolls down the final steps.

When the child failed to stop the ball, or was destined not to, and his friend couldn't either (only one person at a time can go down the steps), the ball seemed lost. The damp steps cast a ramp to the left and another to the right to lessen the slope, but the ball went straight, hit a corner, soared, and at the bottom—this had never happened before—it went over the railing with a mocking leap, stopping beyond the tracks.

It was a winter day, year XIV of the fascist era, or 1936, or maybe it was the year before? The boy went back to the square to pick up his jacket and Gino picked up his, too. He always did everything like his friend. It was too late to play again. The evening devoured the colors of Sanremo, all the way up into the woods beyond Our Lady of the Coast; the sky scraped its belly against the broken cliffs. It was not at all colder than the other days, only without a ball, the sweat froze on his neck.

The child put his hands on the railing. It was relatively low, two meters long, made of iron, freshly painted, green and cold and shiny like the tracks. The other child had followed him.

The child said, "I'll go get it." He climbed over the railing and jumped onto the gravel.

The other child leaned over and this time, did not follow him. He only managed to say, "You're crazy, you can't cross the tracks."

The child below explained that he did not cross them. He looked at the gravel, at the crossties (in his mind, he called them rails), named everything he looked at, and counted the steps that separated him from the ball.

On the long spaces of the railroad, the daylight had not yet faded like elsewhere.

"I'll go where they end, and I'll come back and get the ball. That's not so hard, is it?" he said to convince himself.

Then, as if he had forgotten, he added the most important thing: "Before going all the way around again, I'll throw it to you."

The other child waited.

With his back toward the light cut out by the frontier, the child moved a few steps toward the hills to the east, taking his hands out of his pockets right away because the gravel slid under his foot and he needed to be careful. He predicted that every so often, a train would arrive and the spaces would shrink.

When it happened the first time, the child realized that the train was a long, iron heart, and he soon learned to keep his eyes closed because the dust is a bastard. From then on, every step would be dictated by the anticipation of the scare.

Beyond the tracks, there are a few houses and the black void beyond the roofs should be the sea, but the child doesn't care about the void. On this side of the tracks, between the gravel and the wall, a groove opens up just deep enough for him to hurt himself; ivy grows there, so even if a few floodlights are lit along the tracks, he cannot see where he puts his left foot. The wall is made of stone, all red and dusty, and the child doesn't know if it's the delayed effect of the sunset or the color of rust that has taken over the gravel and stone, or if it depends on the floodlights. He reaches down and touches the track. It is perfectly smooth and cold; in the summer, it might be boiling hot. When he turns to see if Gino is still waiting by the railing, he no longer sees him. The ball is still there, far away, across the tracks, exactly where it was. Hopefully no one will snatch it. Maybe Gino isn't there anymore because the tracks have curved slightly and the profile of the houses covers the uphill outline of the boundary cliffs? *Probably*, he says to himself.

He could turn back around. He would then understand that dreams should not be pursued at all costs. It is necessary to give them up now, before it seems too late. He could not be told these things; he would ignore them for a long time. But if he knew that his mind, for the rest of his life, would try at all costs to return to everything his eyes grazed this evening, he would now make sure to not forget anything.

The tracks thread through a tunnel and the child, lifting his collar and pulling it up with his nose, takes a few steps inside, smells all that cold air, and feels unsure. The space between the wall and the tracks has shrunk—just a little, but it has—and the darkness scares him.

Tardetti, the word old people use in Bresca Square, which Angiolina tells them when she opens the shutter to make them stop kicking balls against her house. Isn't it *tardetti*, kid?

Will it soon be the same outside as inside? No, not even the darkness of a medieval wash house is as dark as a tunnel. What awaits him in a tunnel? Can an animal hide there?

Probably, he says to himself.

So he decides to climb up the ridge beside the tracks, clinging to the gorse, unsure of whether they'll hold. He finds a fence and climbs over it, until the night finally catches him and he can no longer see where he puts his footing. Then he stops; he is hungry, cold, and his jacket is not enough to keep him warm. He sleeps for a while against an olive tree trunk, disturbed by the rattling and pulsing underground. In the belly of the mountain, there is a continuous passing that makes the earth and the stones and the bark and the grass tremble. His heart wrenches. But where is he going, to retrieve a ball? Is he sure he wants to keep going? Why doesn't he answer these questions?

Chills wake him. He calls out for his mother and is surprised when he does. So many times in the last few hours the desire to do so has gripped him, to look for her, as one breathes, as one hopes for the end of a toothache. And now that he has done so, he says, "Oh Mama," and smiles because in all this darkness, she is present. And now Gino would tease him.

He squeezes his eyes shut and reopens them too often to see reality. It is no longer night as before; it is already getting clearer and the grass, by dint of looking at it, has turned gray again and then green. The image of the olive tree bark being plowed tells of a growing discomfort.

A mouse watches him from the last line of stones. Is it a mouse?

The child thinks of one thing: Will there be a little mouse every night to stand guard like a little soldier? If someone comes, will the little mouse warn him?

The child looks at the volume of the valley. Nothing today can be what it was and slowly, in order to forget, he can go back to sleep and tell himself that nothing is real. When he wakes up, it is the following day, but it had been for a while.

He touches his jacket and it is soaked, yet it has not rained. He does not know the names of things—the first humidity of the day, which is followed by dew, and up until now, he did not even know hunger. He continues climbing up again, and once at the top, he has to descend the slope back east, until he finds the tracks again. He had to look for them for a long time, for he could not find them; in the meantime, he had even deluded himself that he would discover the end of them and that he had quickly figured it out. He imagined his mother's distressed smile, and Gino's astonishment at seeing him again with the ball. But then, as he descended almost to the coast, the sight of the tracks proceeding uniformly to the east and west threw him back into despondency. Hunger does the rest. It is not vegetable season, and only some leafy greens grow in the gardens; four apples have fallen from a tree—the last—a couple of which are not quite yet rotten. He learns to take the rot out of the fruits to get a few edible bites, to never again delude himself, ever, when the tracks seem to disappear into a tunnel because, sooner or later, they will come alive again. And so his uncertain passage over the gravel teaches him the tricks of his new railroad life, and the rustle of his jacket keeps him company. But why does he choose east? Couldn't he chase the sunset? Evening, he knows, would come later.

And so, day after day, he climbs over the collapses, crosses villages, olive groves, and forests composed of other plants, and meets farmers who give him an apple. When he is alone, he finds pleasure in noticing the light that strips the sea, the announcement and smell of rain in the air, and every time he sees the tracks coming out of the pierced cliff, he knows that after a while, a train will pop up and the silence will be torn by a thousand balls against the glass. If he calls out "Oh Mama," he no longer hears a train pass over his heart. Yet he calls for her every night, and some nights, he falls asleep watching the toad's sad face, born with the rain, numb, and warms it with his child breath.

ARMA DI TAGGIA STATION

The cities whose stations and benches he got to know, the little mice who stood guard at arm's length and those who balanced on the gleaming tracks at night and noticed him only at the last second, the public gardens where he slept, the *carabinieri*[2] from which he escaped– all these adventures no longer count.

The first station had a double name: Arma di Taggia. He was a child and there was a young girl, or rather she was still a child herself, but didn't look like one anymore. She had asked him where he was going and he had said where they end, blinking in the direction of the tracks. She said, "Where are you going, dummy?" and he replied, "It's true." He had a commitment to attend to and now it was too late to stay there. "Come on, it's late, go home," she said. They had talked for a while; she had shared a focaccia with him. At a certain point, he had thanked her and said he had to go now.

The blue, mournful darkness of the nights and the odorous darkness of the tunnels were now less frightening. If the light at the end could be glimpsed from the entrance, he knew it could be done quickly. If he felt his iron heartbeat, he did not have to try to reach the light at all costs, just throw himself onto the gravel.

In Arma di Taggia, a long time before, when he was more of a child than he is now, on the morning when the little girl had shared a focaccia with him, a train had stopped beside him and he had practiced. Lying on the gravel, he had calculated that the platform protruded, but if the space was an arm's length, it could be done.

"Get up dummy, everyone pees there," she told him.

A railroad worker said, "What are you doing, are you crazy?" No, he wasn't, not at all, he just wanted to take measurements. He had to be sure.

"What are you laughing at?" she had asked him.

Now when he would throw himself on the platform beside the gravel and the train would pass, he would smell the odor of urine. Then

---

[2] Italian military police force

silence would return, and he would stand there a little longer, and he would laugh, because he knew very well that trains never pass by one after the other.

The tunnels saved him quite a few trips around the hills, but they had to be short—tunnels from here to there—to be rushed through in seconds, otherwise he would not venture, and if next to the gravel he could not count on a sidewalk, he would not go into it, not even if he knew that to get there he would have to take some unpleasant Piedmont route, as he called the railroads that led inland.

In the meantime, he was becoming familiar with the method of hill shortcuts and the barracks scattered at high altitude. In reality, they were not really hills; in the third grade, his teacher called them that, but the hills in the subsidiary were soft and green, while these only worked longways, repetitively, like a train, articulated aspects of a degrading world. Boring ridges, composed of a truckload of terraces, one behind the other, with the small central rainwater conduit, dividing and barring the roadway like a railroad crossing.

Some lands were inhabited, others less so, and broken by cuttings and cliffs. At twilight, the stony grounds stirred in a flickering light, the whole valley looked like a mane of stone in the wind, and green and blue things grew there.

One day he had looked in the mirror and, apart from the hair he knew reached his shoulders like a woman's, he had discovered a dry face full of dirty pimples. He found that the countryside was transforming like his face, becoming more and more infested with greenhouses and construction sites.

Not even the dominating blue of the olive trees, however, could be said to have served to make that place resemble a hill because hills are supposed to be pyramid-shaped, to be the things dreamed of by the pharaohs, and he knew this well from having learned it in school with Gino. No, Liguria, at least almost as far as Alassio, where he would arrive sooner or later, that year or in a few years—it doesn't matter—was an example of an obstacle course, full of waves, one on top of the other. Maybe on the other side, where the sun fell, in the direction he had not chosen, there were hills. But he had not gone there, and now what was there was not there. If he could have chosen again, he would have liked to go to Piedmont, which he heard about from the pickers in Oltre Tanaro, who toiled in the olive trees. They would share a piece of bread and oil with him and scold him, in their dialect, ordering him to go home. His mother would have died of a broken heart.

Piedmont was supposed to be a place with that name and dialect. There were rivers, not thin, high-flowing streams, and then the beauty of Piedmont was that a region with that name was supposed to present itself with real mountains and hills. But there was a problem: from Sanremo to Savona, there were no tracks, as far as he knew.

These discussions meant for peers, and the question of the sunset, had been confusing him lately. He would check the sun's slide in the evenings, and now that he was approaching Alassio and would arrive there sooner or later, that year or who knows when—it didn't matter—it seemed to him that the light was coming down from around Sanremo, while in Sanremo he remembered seeing the sunset far to the west. Life and sunsets were a trick.

How many winters had passed since the night he played with Gino and they had lost the ball.... Every time a winter passed, a summer also passed, and what mortified him was this alternating heat and cold and rain and sickness like any bunch of tracks he happened to find here and there, waiting to be reused. He would have liked to reuse time. To know its trick, like he had learned not to be fooled by the sunset.

AROUND THE DIANO MARINA STATION

On the hills between Mount Calvario, Mount Parasio, and Cape Berta, he stopped for a while. From the greenhouses at the top, one could see the sea foam collapsing onto more sea foam and finally onto the beaches, but it was another trick and the subterranean waves somehow had to slowly rise up the slope, otherwise sooner or later, the water would run out. Sometimes the elevation of the horizon seemed right at Mount Calvario's height, just a stone's throw away. Then, if it woke, Corsica would explode, stretch, and elongate spaces and dreams, and the moonlit corridors would yawn all the way into the next night.

During the winter, after sunset, he would enter the greenhouses and in the shelter, he would find an ancient warmth. If they had not recently used pesticides and fertilizers, in the clean warmth, his mother's smell impregnated that of the timber, and he thought of her sniffing the earth and the stretches of grass between crops, and then lowered his eyelids. He didn't mind feeling guilty, that way he could resent being the son who left for a ball. One should not stray far for a ball, no son should do so without giving anyone notice. He called himself by name—no one had called him that in years—and wondered if regretting it meant not paying for it after all. Probably.

The owner of the greenhouses had given him some t-shirts and a pair of leggings, so he could throw away certain things that were ruined. He had saved a flap of one of his old t-shirts as a souvenir—he liked museums. He let him stay in the shelter and in the morning, he shared breakfast with him. One day, he told him, if he wanted to work, there was work for him; he could continue the threshold of a wall, in the terraces of the uncultivated greenhouse, which had collapsed the year before. It was a matter of extracting the stones—he taught him how to use the spike and bident—separating the good stones from the chippings, splitting roots and tracing a threshold thirty centimeters wide and seventy deep, with a slight curve like the tracks in Sanremo.

When he was tired, he would lie down in the threshold as if he were in a pit and feel his sweat drip, gazing at the sky through broken glass. There was not a soul around on that illuminated ridge, except for the owners of the greenhouses, and in the rose gardens, the stray dogs and cats. But a few ridges east, petanque players would gather there on Sundays, and he would go to watch. He liked to hear the metallic clack of the bowls in the wind. The trains passed a few terraces down and covered all other sounds.

One day, the owner's wife came to bring breakfast and set her eyes on him. She came back the next day well-combed and wearing lipstick; the owner noticed and, at the end of the day, made up an excuse and said there would be no more threshold work for a while. Since a compensation was never agreed upon but every now and then, the owner would give him some money to go down and buy a big bottle of wine, he was paid what he was paid and he accepted without protest.

He resumed walking along the tracks, and in Diano Marina, on Via Roma, he bought two iron bowls, paid a few liras for them, and put them in his backpack. They weighed more than a spike and sometimes he felt like throwing them down a cliff, but when he found a clearing beside the tracks, he liked having them with him. He would bowl for a whole day, back and forth, try a shot, fail the bowl, go pick it up, and try again. Then one day–he was almost at Andora–he hit three bowls in a row and even managed a *picchetto*[3]. Then he sat and looked at the sea beyond the pines and wished he could lie down in the shade beside the rose farmer's wife.

He took off the backpack that he found on a cliff, which he always carried over his shoulder–he had abandoned his old, ruined backpack on a bench, and not even his jacket, tight and ragged, had fit him properly in years–held everything in his hand to run better, and threw himself in the dark, in a drizzling rain, on the ground made uncertain by the gravel. He was full of wounds and bruises he got from falling and hitting the tracks with dead weight, and the deep abrasions on his knees were from when he made them taste the gravel, the embankments, the shards of glass. The scrapes could be dangerous, caused by rusted iron wire, nails, pieces of an electro-welded mesh that had only

---

[3] A picchetto occurs when a bocce ball hits another bocce ball and takes its place.

recently been introduced in Liguria and had already rusted. Or simply barbed wire, crosslinked for climbing over to steal a few oxheart tomatoes, his favorites.

The first part of the tunnel before the twilight zone and then the rest to follow, faintly lit by floodlights and populated by flying bats, spiders, and salamanders, reminded him of the ancient longing for darkness, of Gino's words, "If they let us go to the movie theater one day, I want to go in the tunnel." No longer his timber of voice, only the words and images, the days spent with him, in the memory of a world flayed by Corsica's light.

All he retained of his mother was the timber of her voice. Her smell he had not found on any human, in any garden, reedbed, station.

In a greenhouse long ago, in the wooden scaffolding, he had smelled the changing rooms at the Bagni Paradiso. As for movies, he had never been in a movie theater again.

Time passed, full of the same constants: early in the morning, a nightingale woke him up and Corsica welcomed him. That song fooled him; he imagined a bird full of color, but instead, these nightingales were the color of the earth when it hasn't rained for months. Blackbirds, a dark and shiny plumage; he also liked their repertoire. If their beaks were as black as their feathers, they were young and dumb, but when their beaks turned yellow, they possessed the sumptuousness of their song and one day, they would get shot by hunters. Often, he would find their corpses in the middle of the tracks.

Some seasons it always rained, and in the tunnels, the available spaces allowed for side paths; he would go through them out of curiosity or the need to rest, and sooner or later, the train would surprise him. The displacement of the air reached into the crevices. He recognized the freight cars because they usually released grain dust. Sometimes he would get so lost in the depths that he would spend whole days looking around everywhere, and when he came out, the light hurt him. The aquifers fascinated him, giving rise to sounds. He would consume the flashlight battery in there, study the stalactite formations, and stay there–if they were not sewers–sitting on a stone, as one pauses to hear the nightingale after sunrise. The State Railroad workers used the spaces nearest to them as tool shelters–shovels, spikes, lumber, pieces of rail, materials difficult to transport–knowing full well that those kinds of places were frequented by the homeless and runaways, and anything of value would disappear.

In there, he happened to meet characters like himself, and he would stop and talk in the dark (they would sometimes be Slavs and then they wouldn't understand each other) or in front of the flame of a small bonfire, and everyone would recount a piece of their destiny– *destiny*, an exaggerated word–their adventures, and after their discussions, they would take long sips of wine. He, too, would tell his story. His strange world written, invented, he believed, by a writer who had shared his city of residence with him–not his city of birth–and returned to it from time to time. He was someone who had been living in Turin for years now, writing and reading for a major publisher, and was said to have become a very intelligent man. How did he know these things? Did he intuit them? Can one guess matters of fate? No, but one still believes to know them, understand them, he would tell his peers, and sometimes, he would change his mind. In fact, if one night it was a writer who invented him, other times it was an actor, a sailor, someone who watched the Ligurian coast and was bored, or a singer at the Sanremo Music Festival. It was God who had invented him. How calmly this name resounded. If long ago, Christ had found a railroad instead of a lake shore, wouldn't he have walked along the tracks? They listened to him.

But the writer, at that point, was really there and it was on this detail that he based his theories, sank his reasons. He had taken to going to the library in Diano Marina, sleeping at night in the shack, in a field of artichokes (just below was a barrack and he feared he would be recruited or even arrested for desertion), and after discovering the books of so many people from Liguria and Piedmont, and that Italo Calvino from Sanremo, one day that he had promised himself he would leave the town of Diano behind, he learned a fundamental detail. To a childhood friend, a certain Duilio, Italo Calvino had told the story of a child who was looking for the end of the tracks.

And that day, after reading every detail, the railroad man was brought to tears. No longer a lifelong child or even a boy, he was shaving and cutting his hair at stations with a razor he had found in an abandoned piece of luggage. And on seeing this vagabond weep over the pages of Duilio Cossu, the Diano Marina library employees were moved; one even shared lunch with him. He asked if he could copy the article—it was a long article that talked in depth about Italo Calvino and his railroad invention—and the librarian provided him with a pen and paper.

The following fragment can be reproduced as a testimony:

> It all began with the story of a child playing with a ball and that ball ended up over the railroad tracks. The child naturally wants to get it back but his mother warns him not to cross the tracks, because crossing the tracks is dangerous. The child obeys his mother and goes in search of the end of the tracks, crossing green valleys, fertile plains, and arid steppes, arriving at distant lands, among men with unrecognizable faces.

While transcribing, he had asked for a dictionary and looked up the meaning of "fertile." They had forgotten to mention Gino and the old Tuscan man's threats promising to puncture their ball. And Angiolina, resigned to keeping the shutters closed.

The librarian invited him to return, to read Calvino—she loved him too—to have tea with her, and, after that invitation, he tells his fellow vagabonds, an idea of luxury had crossed his mind: a bowl of soup and a hot bath in the young lady's house. But the librarian smiled a little, not realizing his intentions and continuing to beg him, "Come, I mean it, come to the library, to read Calvino."

Actually, Italo Calvino's books don't convince him at all, he briefly explains to everyone. He picks them up as soon as they come out, sits down at the library table, and after a while, he sighs and stops reading. He never gets much out of them, though he recognizes great intelligence and things that concern him, like images of islands that could be Corsica, or floating, resurfaced slabs. Shacks, delusions. The usual stuff of writers.

He never took notes and did not jot down a single bibliographical statement; he simply found the latest on Calvino once a year in the library like the tracks at the station. But that time, he had transcribed every last one of Duilio Cossu's words in his third-going-on-fourth-grader handwriting, and now, not a day went by that he did not go back over those few words to convince himself of how it had gone.

He read the fable to me on a bench in Corso Imperatrice one morning while on vacation, and he read it with a warmth that I did not know from him.

So, on that June afternoon in 1940, we walked through a city we would never see again. We were not cheerful, even though school had ended early that year. At the front that ran just beyond Ventimiglia and just before Menton came the roar of Italian and French artillery, and we went to the pier, to hear the bursts better and perhaps see the flashes better. The sun sent waves of warmth and light over the beaches and hills of Sanremo, and some fishermen were intent on pulling barnacles off the rocks. The profile of Cape Nero flickered in the glare.

Apart from this coincidence, when they asked him why it had to be Calvino who had invented him, he could not answer. He just felt it. It was him, certainly, more than anyone else, more than some actor, more than some sailor. It was him.

Not much can be said about the time of the release of the Cossu interview; rumors differ, some claimed he had given the interview in the 1950s or early 1960s, others much later. But he had read that story in Diano and later found it in the preface of a book in Alassio.

From time to time, his supposed inventor would also cross Liguria by train, and who knows, they might have met somewhere. For a moment, Calvino would have crossed his eyes without recognizing him, the dog who, after so long, ignores the being he conceived, but somehow knows it is him? Literary fate.

And he would have liked to meet him, oh, he would have liked it even if Calvino, when questioned and cornered, had denied paternity. In any case, grab something with the writer at the zinc counter of a café at the station in Alassio or Laigueglia, Albenga. It was one of those questions that they did not fail to ask him down there, and he would lower his eyelids.... To meet him or meet him again. After all, they were about the same age, and it was not certain that they had not frequented the same alleys in Sanremo or the little square where the wagoners parked.

He had become fond of these things in the Cuban-born writer's biography by accident, for the pleasure of sharing a geography, and also because the library tables were always full of his books, and all they talked about were half viscounts and nonexistent knights.

If Cossu's article had been transcribed before 1958, he had a suspicion that everything may have been true when he found *The Baron in the Trees* in the bookstore. Calvino had published it the year before, with the same publisher he usually worked for. That winter afternoon, having finished reading it, the railroad man looked up at the window of the Laigueglia library and smiled. *Come on…someone who invents a rampant baron cannot have failed to create someone like you sooner or later.* He demonstrated maniacal perfection: the same handful of constraints, the sea as seen from Ombrosa, the different point of view, the verticality, on the one hand; the Pigna and Bresca Square, the rolling balls and the tracks on the other…because someone like that, someone like Calvino, must have known the peculiarities of Liguria like the back of his hand.

That time, too, he sought help in the words of a random librarian, getting near her and whispering the matter to her. "What else could trigger, ma'am, his obsession with the vegetation's verticality, if not a form of counterbalance such as railroad mineral horizontality…." He had studied the words for hours, satisfied and expecting a compliment, but the librarian smelled him and quickly ruined his moment, tilting her head to one side and returning only a whispered "Oh my."

He sat back down, smiling and blissful, and yet, at the same time, a little bitter about that end that Calvino gave Cosimo. He could have made peace with the earth again, but no, instead, he stood there looking at those dirty library windows, imagining the hot air balloon, the dangling rope to which Cosimo was clinging, heading toward the sea of Genoa, pass by at any moment in that piece of the Laigueglia sky…. Had his creator reserved such an end for him as well? An end in which he spends his life chasing the end of the tracks and eventually boards a train like Cosimo in his hot air balloon amid the lightning.

But then, what was the use of knowing? Did knowing change any-thing? He would ask his friends at the bivouac, and he would tell them it doesn't matter, and because it didn't matter, they would end up drinking to it. Nobody judged him, not down there, not like elsewhere that when he finished talking they would laugh. At that point, the ball must have simply been deflated, discolored, punctured; by now, he knew all the jokes by heart.

Everyone carried their own ghosts with them, and as for him, he was tired of pointing out that, in the end, it was not even a matter of balls anymore. One would go on, and go on going on, like in a factory, on shift, and in the end, before the wine, one would silently divide with the residents of the dark the things put together for lunch. He had gotten himself another backpack–his third or fourth–because his last had been stolen some time ago, and he had borrowed this one from a shed next to a greenhouse, one of those places that smelled like pesti-cides and was more contaminated than tunnels. One day, he would take it back to where he got it. Perhaps he was still a child.

Around Cape Mele

Inside a tunnel, under the faint light of a floodlight, he had found a rusty bolt the size of a mandarin, and put it in his pocket.

The refugees of the tunnels would wipe their mouths, take a sip, and hand him the carton, and he had learned to do the same. The first time, his head spun and he fell asleep in the cave, but then he learned how to dose and only his head spun.

After all, he noticed that he was no longer a young man in his attempt to measure spacetime: not by the number of years he frequented the tracks, but by the number of towns he had passed, stations and escarpments and clearings, more or less habitable hills, and how he stopped everywhere for a single hour or month, or two months, or several seasons. How he arrived with the long rains before the heat and left before the next summer or the one after. The city with two stations, for example, and its classification yards, its piles of train rails, its mountains of gravel already rusted before it was even laid out. By how much he had left himself behind the dead tracks of Port Mauricio and Oneglia.

Nothing to get excited about, many bundles of tracks—one, two, even three—continued parallel. And before these calculations he would come to a halt again and, taking a pause between the tired, disappointed man and the daydreamer on a bench, he would end up lying down and falling asleep in the sun. He would squeeze his eyes shut and in the fire of his iris, he would see his mother again.

Construction crews and bulldozers broke hillsides, casting gigantic bridges—no one had ever seen such imposing ones—and when the bulldozers and workers left after a few hot and dusty seasons, motorcycles, buses, and faster and faster cars and trucks began to pass over those bridges and overhanging roads, and on the hills where he rested, watching the sea foam from afar, the roars muffled even the sound of the trains.

In the buzz coming from the beaches of Diano Marina, San Bartolomeo, Cervo, Andora, Laigueglia, Alassio (how beautiful Alassio was), all the way after Albenga, he would always hear her voice, her words that became one with the sea, the voice that knew how to bring him back to the Bagni Paradiso.

"Mom, I'm going in the water."

"Not where your toes don't touch the bottom."

It was her.

"Mom, I'm going to play ball."

"Okay, but don't sweat."

In the water, that world in which he could not touch the bottom with his toes was the entire world, the path. Her voice emerged from the shores, or from further away, coming from the little islands that the coast disseminated between her eyes and the horizon. The fierce colors, scattered by the day and burned by the moon. Sometimes at dawn, the wrecks of the barges appeared out of nowhere, slipping on diamonds; even those colorful barges were rocks, and his mother, devoured by her own dreams and guilt, materialized at the bottom. The unreachable island, a kind of Corsica hanging on the horizon, which you never know if it is there, if it is land or sea, but you know it is no longer there. The only voice with no more matter, a pier in the blue void, resting on the seabed and floating at the same time, the mission and illusion of being a bridge for no one. Life then was as if it was biting itself off the shore, and lingering off the *stempo*[4]. He missed his mother so much that he would have swam to her, if he knew how to swim....

He tried to learn at the Bagni Paradiso once, but then the next winter, he had set out to retrieve the ball. *Is that what happened? Probably,* he told himself.

Italo Calvino had also surveyed at length the sea from the mountains opposite Corsica. It happened when he was a young man and a partisan. And did he and Walter Benjamin ever see each other again? No, the last time they saw each other was that time at the Sanremo station. After that, Benjamin left and returned to Liguria the following year, while Italo's father recruited his sons and asked them to help him in the San Giovanni countryside and in the greenhouses, so that by watching Libereso, they would learn something. And still, there was more to it, there

---

[4] This is a word invented by the author to describe the course of the railroad man's private life.

was the fact that that year, Italo was of age and preferred to go to the movie theater with Duilio and Eugenio and other boys.

As for Walter, he was a man hunted by shadows and would be forever. That last time, at the station, Italo had only been able to say a few things to him, leaving everything up in the air. Although, they must have been important discussions and questions, such as, where was the suitcase? Duilio had asked him that too, seeing that he did not have it with him. This bespectacled, hunched-backed man from the north carried only his backpack over his shoulder, along with the small trunk he had with him when he arrived and the porter had unloaded for him. In other words, were the children's picture books left in Villa Verde?

A few years later, Walter Benjamin had begun his extreme journey, and the last place he had lived in was a room in a guesthouse at the foot of the Pyrenees. In this journey, one is also destined to talk about a lost suitcase. What had the man with no more land to escape to thought about that night? The drawings of the islands? The green and blue colors of the ocellated lizard?

Following these events, fighting began in Sanremo—as everywhere in Italy—and it was a fierce war. Italo had taken refuge in a hiding place filled with people; it was like being in a tunnel without trains. The boots of the Nazis and fascists crunched on the paved streets. Italo had his suspicions about the books' whereabouts, and one day down there, talking to a waiter who had been in Mrs. Dora's service at Villa Verde for a long time, he learned that the leather suitcase full of picture books was still in the basement of the boarding house.

Before going up the mountain, he had been to Villa Verde and had revisited the garden, a bit like when a season rolls around again. That world told of surrender, uncultivated and abandoned as it was, the dry leaves of the palm trees hiding the sea. He had talked to the janitors and though the villa was temporarily closed for work, Dora had moved—no one knew where. To England, someone said, with her son, who was also Walter's son. Of the suitcase, no news.

In the mountains, he had met the son of a wagoner. Italo often made friends among the sons of muleteers, and this man had told him that just before he went up the mountain, he had helped his father move furniture and entire bookcases from villas owned by Jews in

Sanremo and the surrounding areas. They had also picked up and transported items from Villa Verde. He remembered it vividly. A few things, a few chairs, a bed, a few suitcases, everything piled up in an old tinderbox. What was useful was sold, the rest was burned. Everyone knew full well what happened to the Jews' things.

After the war, Italo had gone back to look for the suitcase, but each time less, in the sense that he no longer had hope, as rumors spoke of the inevitable bonfire fueled by all the papers and things of little value left without owners. By that time, after university, Italo had moved away for good, the flat, geometrically perfect streets of Turin had replaced the alleys, and the sense of Ligurian verticality would survive only in his pages and in his imagination.

All he could do was read everything Walter had time to write and not lose, and to be pleased that it was the same publishing house he worked for that would publish his work. Thus, the question of whether Walter Benjamin had a secret suitcase with him in the Pyrenees had arisen. But some said it had later been found, even though, according to others, some of its contents had been lost forever.

Every now and then, Italo would go back to Sanremo and meet with Duilio, who had since become a lawyer and Eugenio, his other very good friend, who had become a brilliant journalist. Together they would sit on the benches on Corso Imperatrice, like they used to do as children. Who knows, maybe he would mention the fable about the end of the tracks. Maybe they would look at Corsica together in silence, as if that silence contained everything from their childhood and adolescence: the swims at the wreck, the war, the San Giovanni countryside, the fables about the balls, the incredible encounter with Benjamin, and the barely missed encounters with the blue lizard.

More than anything, they talked about an Italy that was still battered, the things that were important to think about, the state of those things, how to maintain freedom and democracy and understand the blood of the victors and the vanquished. From Italo, they wanted to know what people were reading, and about Paris, where he had gone to live at one point, about the house in Tuscany he wanted to buy and the land in Sanremo he would soon sell with his brother. About the family books he was going to donate to the Civic Library.

One day, he and Duilio had gone to watch the sea, in that stretch after the Monumental Cemetery of the Foce, and passing Villa Verde, they had looked up at the palm trees. Usually, all conversation ended in that room full of death, in the Port Bou inn, and everything else was forgotten. But that time, down there in front of the sea, Duilio said, "The fable about the child and the ball...."

"And the tracks...and the boy and the islands. I regret not writing it. I could always do it."

"You know, it's just that there really is a child looking for the end of the tracks...."

Since Italo said nothing, Duilio slowly began again.

"He is probably our age, give or take a year."

Italo let out a chuckle, and immediately became serious again. Duilio informed him of the details, leaving nothing out—this story was the talk of the town. Even though he had been missing for years, it was still strange to him that he had never heard it, but Italo had an excuse, he hardly hung out with anyone in Sanremo anymore, except his mother and close friends.

The railroad boy's mother gave piano lessons and his father had been dead for years—the child had hardly known him. He was a normal child, but some said something was off about him. One day, the ball had climbed over the railing in Bresca Square, and ended up on the tracks. The child was stubborn, and through who knows which way, had set out to retrieve the ball. They knew nothing else except that his mother had followed his trail, toward the east, the direction indicated by his playmate who had last seen him.

Sanremo. Italo would have received only slaps from the city, sold his father's land, seen buildings spring up like mushrooms, and perhaps that horizontal story was only worth the effort of being told to invent the life of a boy who, so as not to disobey his mother, had obeyed literature.

And so that day, Italo Calvino watched the sea. It was around noon and Corsica was far, far away—it had been hours since he last saw it—and maybe it would emerge at sunset, maybe not. And Calvino watched it anyway.

AROUND ANDORA

Corsica is the place where dreams burn at dawn, Calvino claimed, but he had never known this Calvino, as a child or as an adult, and Calvino's Corsica was not his Corsica. Perhaps they resembled each other, as islands do. His Corsica was just the fragment of a drift, a ship destined to sink in some invisible sea (of time?). For it is not like islands are eternal; they are there and then they are gone.

Some nights, the railroad man would talk about Corsica with fellow travelers. He was the one who brought it up; to the others, it had always been just a distant thing. The Corsican island. Then everyone would say their piece. The cathedral before the ravine. Things like that.

Sometimes he was silent too, blaming fever and hunger, but he did not stop thinking about the futility in the air, about Corsica and who had invented it. He ignored all of this; no, not even he knew anymore how he had stumbled into this wandering life of his. He wanted freedom and freedom existed only through the worship of freedom. The fever made him lose his mind, and so he would lie a whole day on the benches of a station, sweating, until the fire went out and passed, like a train over his heart, leaving marks. Meanwhile, among those passing by the bench—usually some pitying women—there was always someone willing to spare a coin and place it in his cap.

He stayed around Andora for a long time—maybe a year—working on the beach, cleaning and raking the sand at night, keeping the coins that people lost around the beach chairs; there were a lot of them, a tip of sorts.

At night, they allowed him to sleep in a large shack filled with rags, nets, shovels, and life jackets, and during the day, they asked him to leave the shack free and clean.

He still read, an alibi for warming himself in libraries during the winter. He liked one in fifty books, and since there were thousands in there, he would start them all and if he didn't like them, he would drop them almost immediately. Sports newspapers, on the other hand, he would read from cover to cover even if they were about stupid things, about soccer. In fact, he was crazy about things like that. He could hardly explain certain oddities to himself.

The boy who walked along the tracks was infinitely distant, lost in an unfamiliar railroad system, or one that preceded him. Either way, in some respects, he had remained the boy who played games along the tracks. Now and then, he thought about these games—the huts made of branches, the Native Americans' hideouts and assaults on the train like in the Western movies—and the child too, and the difference between childhood and the rest of railroad life lay exactly in that pretense of playing seriously.

Besides games, if there was anything else he had managed to engage in thoroughly during childhood, it had been that constant looking around, keeping himself ready, sensing danger before it arrived. Life fueled by luck, that was how it had gone so far. As a boy, he had managed to shelter himself from the war, to hear its gunfire, to see the dead in the streets and stations, and to not go mad. To not starve to death. To run away from the bombs and find people crushed in the tunnels. The smell of fires and dust raised by collapses made him think of the mountains too, but it would have meant giving up everything.

And now that he was an adult and the fevers ended, he got up with difficulty, sore, and went to wash his neck and teeth at the station. Staring at himself in the mirror, he realized that he had escaped only by some trick, like the law of sunsets, the mysteries of islands, a form of *stempo* that governed literary lives.

His long beard, a few white strands, were just a detail that could give him chronological news, while the rest, the cascade of ivy and vines and flowers and agaves, welded to the karst wall on which he leaned as hard as he could to keep from getting sucked into a train, belonged to a kind of logic, a flawed railroad logic. No, nothing about life could be explained, really nothing. Maybe there was a formula, but it had to be a formula that was as unknown, at least to him, as the stars and the moon on the tracks could be, or the writing he saw during the day engraved on the rails. Codes that only he noticed and ignored.

Yet there was no hurry, he felt all that flowing as if he were still a child and believed he still had who knows how much of it, at least to finish his work, to give himself credit. And so, almost without realizing it, when he had these unique moments of consciousness and these chills, he would come down the escarpment of the tracks that went inland, look for an underpass, and go to the beach. In his backpack, he always had a pair of shorts. After stripping off everything else, he would lay down on the rocks, and when the sun baked his skin, he would turn over and let himself fall gently into half a meter of water. He would wash the most intimate parts of his body, shaking off the sand as he did at the Bagni Paradiso. He would stay there until sunset, breathing in the salty water and remembering afternoons in the water with his mother and Gino, the shovel, the ball....

One day, thinking about all these things, he pretended to know how to swim, and after a while, he noticed that he was floating. That day, he saw a deflated ball among the rocks, reached out his hand, and as if he were a crab, retracted it. He felt a bit sad for that useless task of his, all locked into the destiny of chasing nothingness. So, for the rest of the day, to avoid thinking about it, he continued to refine his swimming techniques and everything passed. He was so happy that he had learned to swim that he now felt his mother closer, smelled her, not the violet scent she used before going out, but her motherly smell. And everything passed, even that feeling of well-being, as soon as he got used to the fact that he could swim.

Boats were also passing by offshore, bringing in waves, and with each passage, he felt a throb, and it seemed to him that swimming exerted a kind of throb in his lower abdomen.

From that day on, every time he stopped at a beach to practice, a miracle would occur: the deflated and faded ball would appear among some rocks, and he would feel a little sad again. As if the world were making fun of him. Then he would dry himself off quickly, gather his rags, his belongings, buy a focaccia with his begging change, and head to where he knew.

Actually he couldn't say why he was hurrying back to the tracks. *Maybe because you're tempted to go back to Sanremo? Probably.*

Alassio Beach

One afternoon, immersed in the sandy water, another important thing happened. He thought of himself as one of those people capable of magnetizing stray balls; the boys would play volleyball or kick stationary penalties on the shore, with the goalkeeper in half a meter of water, and sooner or later, the ball would regularly end up in his vicinity. He would pick it up, gauge its consistency–modern, hard rubber balls–and look around to see who to throw it to, nevertheless denying himself the desire to attempt a dribble.

It had already happened several times that afternoon; he returned the ball with his hands and went back to bobbing in his one and a half meter of water, when he noticed that a man, sitting on the rocks, was watching him.

"Your hand is entering the water wrong," said the man. He had strong hair and a calm smile.

"How?"

"Keep your elbow high."

"Like this?"

"Better, but you messed up the arm movement. Your arm must follow your hand's entry into the water…."

"Straight or bent?"

"Straight and then bent. Show me, slowly."

He obeyed, doing about ten very slow strokes, and as his excitement increased, he felt like he was driving a train.

"Keep going, he who stops is lost."

He kept going until he began to spit salt water. He went out and hoisted himself onto the rock, sitting down next to the man who was just standing there, as if he had been put there to check the swimmers' technique.

"Not bad, but you also need to improve your kicks–a matter of practice–and your breathing…."

The sea was the one just past the Coscia Tower; the man had asked him if he was a local. No, he was from Sanremo, and when asked if the sea in Sanremo was no good, he had said yes; the Bagni Paradiso was as good as it gets on the Riviera, but he was not in Alassio for the sea.

The man was not a local either; he owned a house halfway up the coast, was a painter, and liked to move from hill to hill looking for islands. He drew islands and carob trees. He said just that: I am a sketcher of islands and carob trees. And he looked at him to see what it must feel like to hear a stranger say something like that.

The railroad man did not comment and cast a glance at the small island that stood more or less in front of them. Some called it Gallinara, for others it was the island of Alassio.

"Do you draw that?"

"Yes, but that's not the only one, it's never the only one."

To the west, the islet was shaped like a lizard's head and to the east rose the slope of a wooded hill, which in the distance would have looked like a camel's hump, were it not for all that green. At the top of the hump, a few white houses stood out among the foliage, and at the bottom, a clear, rocky strip bordered the island; it must have been the effect of the waves that caused the erosion and absence of vegetation. The yellow strip that wrapped around the island, like dried seaweed, was the most difficult to render on canvas, the man said. It was based on that color there—a dry seaweed shade—although he preferred to work with pencil.

The railroad man looked at the island with a gesture of his chin. This was his way of signaling things; just before, in the same way, he had signaled to him the ball splashing over the waves and bouncing mockingly in front of the goalkeeper.

"It must be nice and cool under all those trees, too bad the seagulls would shit on us," he said. Indeed, more birds were circling in midair around the island than on the entire coast from Alassio to Cape Mele. They were feinting a mass movement toward the coast but, aside from a few direct flights into the sky, most were returning to the island.

"There are always hundreds of them, they will find something to eat," said the man who drew islands. He actually preferred other islets—not as close—although in the end, he drew the islands he came across. For example, the island of Bergeggi was beautiful, and even more so was the island of Albenga, which was actually this one in Alassio, but it was as if there were another island in Albenga, a subject observed from a different angle. This detail, he said, was no small matter, because drawn from elsewhere the same island became another island in all respects. The railroad man listened to his theories, a bit disturbed.

"Did I say something wrong?" said the island man.

The railroad man laughed. "It's just that you talk like some of the books I read in the libraries in Diano and Cervo."

"Cervo. Then you must have seen the Corallini Square. And have you seen the island of Cervo?"

After thinking for a long time about such an eventuality, the railroad man asked if he was sure there was an island or even an islet in Cervo. He had been there a long time ago and had stayed there quite a while, and it seemed to him that he could say that he had never seen anything off the coast of Cervo. He had kept an eye on that sea both from the shore and from halfway up the mountain. There was a beautiful castle and the lady in the restaurant was kind, occasionally giving him a plate of fried anchovies. They hosted galas there and read pages from books. It was summer and maybe the summer haze affected it, but a little island, come on, he would remember it if it had been there.

"In fact, you can't see it, it's actually an archipelago and it's in the waters of Ajaccio. They're called the Sanguinaire Islands."

The railroad man snorted. "Ajaccio is in Corsica," he said, having read about it in an atlas. "All you do is sit on the deck chair in Laigueglia with pencil and paper, feet in the water, and draw the island of Elba. Then you go to Cervo, go up to the square, sit on the steps, draw a few rocks in front of Ajaccio and say they are the islands of Cervo."

The island man nodded, smiling.

"What did you do in Cervo except scrounge anchovies?"

"I don't scrounge anything, dummy."

"I didn't mean to insult you. You must have listened to writers, I imagine they told readers, 'Take a seat and I'll explain life to you.' But they didn't explain that they called it Corallini Square because from the little harbor, boats used to depart en route to the islands. They are islets composed of a stone that takes on a reddish-purple hue at sunset, which must be why they call them the Sanguinaires."

"Were they going there to fish?"

"They were on the hunt for corals, hence the name of the square. Then a misfortunate event occurred and that was the end of coral fishing, but the name remained."

"And every time, you would also draw the Sanguinaires differently?"

"No, I don't see the Sanguinaires, I only change the islands I see."

He not only changed their physiognomy, but he colored them differently. After all, for example, an island in the morning is not the same island in the late afternoon. "Not even close, " he said. It was like seeing a new place.

"Like night and day?" said the railroad man, to follow his absurdities.

"Like night and day," concluded the island man.

"Distant islands, too?"

"Do I draw them? It depends, if I see them, yes, but I just told you, even if I don't see them. To see an island you only need a shade, a cape; every spur that jumps into the sea is an island, not a peninsula. If you look from here towards France, you have the island of Laigueglia, and then that of Cape Mele."

They turned their heads toward the spur of Cape Mele, veiled by vapors and by now, a low sun. That sun entered the sea, and one understood that what it was up to in the water was a miner's job. The island man said the sun transformed porphyrin in coral and sent them to the bottom.

"So Cape Mele looks like an island to you…."

The island man looked at it and said, "Is that a question? Can't you see it's an island?"

He drew those things, polished them, cut them, smoothed the edges, so that from peninsulas, they were forced to become what they were: authentic islands. "Because if you cut off any spur's chin," he said just like that, "its invention is guaranteed," and he made a gesture with his hands as if he had thrown something on the sand.

There were islands toward Genoa too. He pulled out a clipboard from the bag he had with him on the rock, and showed him a map. It was a scribbled map, the entire Ligurian coast, crowded with names and headlands like Cape Noli and, past Genoa, Portofino, and Monterosso, the islands of Tino and Palmaria, all the way to the Tuscan coast.

"The islands of Liguria never end, what do you think, they depend on meteorology; the light, the air, the seasons multiply them."

"Don't you draw anything else?"

"Things I saw years ago, during a forced stay in the south, in a village on top of the badlands. I also really like to draw carob trees, I told you—let me see that."

He had noticed a bad wound on his leg. The railroad man said it was a bump and that half the time in the tunnels, he would fall and hit the ground as if he were in a mine. He said this to make him laugh, but the island man laid his hand on the injured leg and said, "If you want, I can give you something after."

"Are you also a doctor?"

"It's no use laughing. Yes, I am also a doctor."

Every once in a while, they would hear a shout, and the railroad man would turn to look, hop off the cliff, and return the ball.

He had noticed that they didn't do as he and Gino did in Bresca Square, taking turns kicking penalties and free kicks, and whoever didn't score became goalie. At the beach in Alassio, it was always the same goalie. His back to the island, water up to his calves, in the middle of a goal without posts, the ball would bounce at the last second on the wave's crest and mock even the best goalie on the coast.

The island man asked him if he was more interested in the ball than talking about islands, and the railroad man hoisted himself back on the rock and said nothing.

"There are fewer people, show me your breaststroke." But the railroad man said he didn't feel like it; he didn't like to swim breaststroke, and besides, he wasn't used to obeying orders. So they walked to the showers, washed themselves with the bar of soap in the saucer, and each took something more or less clean out of their bags. It took a while for the sun to dry their skin; it was the last sun of the day and it only put effort into its colors. Once they were dressed, saying almost nothing to each other, as if they had agreed upon it long ago, they headed east, appearing to avoid the island of Alassio.

The island man chose a comfortable spot, laid their bags on top of a short wall, and sat down. They did not say anything, but they both knew they were there to await an event.

The island man had taken out binoculars from his bag and was moving them along the horizon. Every now and then, he looked at his watch, and the railroad man laughed.

It would not appear. It was made of wood; at dawn it burned with the dreams of the night, at dusk just a few embers remained among the charred rest. He gathered all his knowledge, recalling words and theories his peers used while sheltered in karst areas. The island man listened to him, but without getting distracted.

He had read about dreams in some library; if he was not mistaken, it was something Calvino affirmed, he said. So for the first time, Calvino's name came up, and the railroad man revealed the possibility that the person behind his railroad journey was Calvino himself.

The island man lowered his binoculars and gave him a sidelong glance.

At a divine time, an old, very traditional Corsica appeared, sitting at one of the most monitored points, and the island man checked the time. He wrote something in a notebook and for a while longer, they were silent.

Almost as if it knew it had been spotted, the island played dumb and sank. Not with the sound of a collapsing cathedral that raises a dust cloud, but suddenly, silently, it had sunk.

How he missed his mother, he told the man.

Was she still alive? She must be, he was barely an adult...of course, if he had outlived her, he could not have gone to her funeral, for he would never have heard about it from anyone...where was his mind going? And the island man—he watched the waves roll in without binoculars—let him ponder.

The silence did not last long, and when the island man looked at the binoculars in the case and put them in his bag, the railroad man took a peek and said, "I would love to see your drawings. They must be interesting, all these different islands."

The island man searched through his bag, pulled out a small extendable easel and another pair of binoculars, which he asked the railroad man to hold, and resumed searching through his folders.

"These look like the ones from the war that the Germans used," said the railroad man, turning the binoculars over in his hands.

"What do you know about wars?"

"I definitely know about wars; I might not know about islands but wars...." he made a gesture with his hand, as if to cut the air. "I was little more than a child when the Germans controlled the stations. If they saw you walking on the railroad, they would shoot you from the windows like mockingbirds; sometimes they would make the train stop and they would get off. Oh, but I would trick them, I would throw myself into a tunnel and lie on the gravel. They would shoot a few times at eye level and would not enter...."

The island man had lit a cigar, filling the air with its scent. He was holding the folder containing his drawings, which he had not yet opened. One could say he was disappointed, he would have liked to show him the drawings, to hear his opinion, not war stories. The railroad man realized this and asked him what he was waiting for.

He took a careful look at them, evaluating sketches of plants that could be pine trees or carob trees, and then moved on to the fish and salami, knives, houses, profiles of old people and children. He also looked inside the pencil case full of colored pencils.

Most were actually drawings of islands, and they were all different from one another, yet the matrix was the same. Twenty, thirty sketches of rocks under which was written, *I. of Diano Marina*, under another *I. of Diano Castello*, *I. of Cervo*, of Laigueglia, Spotorno, Varazze, and other places where he had not yet been, which gave name to a different Corsica.

"The drawings of Diano Castello and Cervo are almost the same, the one of Varazze isn't..."

"Almost isn't the same," said the sketcher.

Under the drawing of Diano Castello, there were three lines of information: viewpoint located between Castello and Varcavello, elevation of about 128 meters ASL. July 29, 1952, 7:20 p.m. Things like that.

"Here is Corsica, as seen from the Taggia Castle one month later. Tell me again if it looks the same?"

The railroad man compared the drawings in either hand.

"Maybe you were the one to draw these differences and insisted on making the ridges of the mountains another color…."

The island man did not let him go on.

"Ridges? What are you saying? I can't refute you because I don't have the photographs here, but my drawings are based on them…and anyway, when you pass Sestri Levante and Lerici, you'll see with the naked eye that the 'edges,' as you call them, are different."

"Who is making you wait for the island? Is someone forcing you to?"

"Who is making me? Let's see, who is making you walk down railroads? The writer from Sanremo? Come on, give me a break."

He looked away, as if he knew more about that story and the writer from Sanremo (he never said Calvino). The railroad man noticed this and changed the subject.

"They would see me coming, and they would keep an eye on me."

"Who are you talking about?"

"I'm talking about the Italian partisans…they knew I was not a spy, and if I informed them about the passage of trains loaded with Germans, they could trust me…." Then he went back to Calvino. "You know, the writer from Sanremo was also a part of the Italian partisans…."

"Yes, I know." That was all he said.

"The suspicion that he is behind all of this—me, I mean—did not come to me after I read his books; at that time, they were not yet in libraries, and he was not yet famous. I don't really know exactly how things went, but I know he was a partisan, and that somewhere, when I would wander around the hills of Imperia as a young man, we might have crossed paths. He would be just a few years older than me. 'If this guy is the one who invented you, whoever he is, then you have his partisan ideas,' I would say to myself…."

The island man struggled to follow him and returned to hinting that he would have preferred to talk about his drawings.

They wandered around Alassio some more, and near the Muretto of Alassio, they stopped to look at certain paintings on display, hands behind their backs. They were Berrino's harbors, which they both liked.

Then they headed uphill to the countryside because the island man had gotten hungry and knew a good place to recharge. He said just that, to recharge.

There was a vegetable garden in the early twilight, and the island man was talking loudly, biting down on his cigar and advancing through rows of tomatoes. Every now and then, he would pluck off and gently put an oxheart tomato in his backpack, but not alongside the drawings; he had pulled out a mesh bag and was filling it. He asked the railroad man to please lend him a hand and grab some too, but he said he wouldn't think of it; if he were caught, he would at the very least get an expulsion order. The island man laughed and kept looting, and every now and then to see if the railroad man was following him, he would call out to him. "Say, expulsion order, are you there?" Or, "What are you doing?"

In fact, the railroad man moved carefully through the vegetables, hunched over, and answered in monosyllables. The less they talked, he said, the better, accustomed as he was to robbing vegetable gardens in silence.

The island man reassured him. "Look, my friend, I've already told you, the vegetable garden belongs to Chicú, a friend of mine. I wouldn't lie to you...."

Needless to say, the railroad man was not at all convinced. Apart from Gino, he had never had a friend. He had worked for farmers, and many times, unfortunately, he had done it for free. Such gratitude. Were those people his friends? He had lived in public places, stations, and tunnels, and had had to surrender to the arrogance of the world, and now he felt a longing for a friend in the garden....

Beyond the crops, a trail divided the new fields, introducing them to a temporarily dusty Alassio. The railroad man proceeded normally, until he came to a halt again and bent over, looking around from behind a tree.

"Shall we see your strange behavior again?"

"We're not doing anything. I won't go beyond there," he protested.

The island man said they were almost home. He told him he lived at the top of the little road to Solva and for dinner, Mrs. Lina would prepare tomatoes for them. He could sleep in a good bed—he had a couple of vacant rooms—and the next day for lunch, she would make them soup.

The railroad man said it was a good proposal, and yet he rejected it.

"Why, let's hear it."

Because he would not cross up there, he pointed with his chin to the railroad. The island man laughed again. "But there's a railroad crossing."

"I don't care." Such frivolity irritated him. "That's how I'll start and then I'll end up crossing it over and over again."

They found a solution, discarding the tracks for an underpass (not the one that had taken him to the beach in the morning), and once across, they were able to go up the steep, little road. Every so often, the island man would turn to look at the tracks and shake his head.

"Everyone has their own obsessions. It's no use laughing, you have the islands, I have the tracks."

Leaving the narrow road for a climb etched into the sides–so much so that at one point, between the rooftops, below, the sea reappeared–they saw signs indicating Solva and the name of a church.

At that point, the railroad man stopped and said, "I don't know where you live, but, to be honest, I don't want to go to your house."

He realized he had been a bit rude. "Let it be known, I thank you for your kindness, but, believe me, it's better that I don't."

The man–his name was Carlo, maybe he had told him a while ago–stopped, put down the bags, folded his arms, and said, "This will be good."

The railroad man tried to clarify one thing right away. No one had ever invited him to eat tomatoes at his home, much less told him that the maid (how did he manage to afford a maid?) would give him a clean shirt. Well, he said, once he met such a human being, he would prefer to say no. "I know full well that something is wrong, but the thing is, I wouldn't want to stray far, that's all."

"From the railroad?"

"Of course, that's what we're talking about."

Carlo found yet another solution. Two hundred meters from the railroad was Chicù's olive grove, with the famous shack. He could sleep up there, bathe–there was plenty of water–and to relieve himself, there was a reedbed.

"You can leave whenever you want, or wait for me and we'll have breakfast together in the morning."

The shack was in the middle of a few dusty olive trees, and all around it were fields lit by a few small lights, and in the sky to the west, some light still held out. Above a little ladder of stones and dirt, there was a wall and tall grass; beggar's lice, or *pidocchi*, as they called them in Liguria, stuck to their pants.

At the bottom of the terrace, the wood and sheet metal shack looked like one of those shelters built in the countryside after the 1887 earthquake.

They sat down. The island man washed the tomatoes under a faucet, and brought two chipped plates from the shack and a half bottle of white wine. First however, he turned on an old flashlight hanging from an olive branch.

"They taste good even if we don't season them."

After cutting the tomatoes, he moved among the plants with his flashlight and returned with three lemons and some basil.

"Put some in your backpack and tomorrow, squeeze them into the water—you know, for vitamins."

The railroad man squeezed some onto the tomatoes, too. "Citrus fruits also cleanse the stomach," he said.

He would not have wanted to get on the topic of the railroad again, but as they ate, the island man asked him, "Say, what kind of life is that? To not be able to stray far from the tracks, doesn't that seem like too much?"

"You're not listening to me. One, I don't cross them—I never will—and two, I don't abandon them. At most, I'll take an underpass, go to the seaside, spend a few days in the countryside, but not for tourism...." He feared falling in love with some place far from the railroad, with a woman, being tempted by a different life.

The island man did not laugh.

For a while, they kept their eyes on the darkness that trampled the cliffs against the sky, no longer saying anything to each other. Fireflies were circling, the corridor of the moon behind them plowed the water. To get a better look at the sea, they had to go and sit on the edge of a low wall that divided the same terrace. There was wood that had been cut and dried years ago.

They talked about Corsica again, as if there were nothing else to talk about.

"You know, after Bergeggi, there are places that offer a viewpoint as if you were seeing it from a thousand meters high. It's indescribable."

"Places? Again with the theory of places...I thought it was just a matter of visibility."

The island man huffed, asking what sense it made to talk about this again, but he repeated a concept. The railroad man stopped him right away. If it didn't seem rude to him, he said, he would rather go and lie down. The island man was indeed offended; he stood up and cleared the table.

The shack smelled of pesticides. The floor was half planks and half dirt, and through the small window came a meager light. The railroad man thought that by lying down he would also see the moon. Was this a trick of angles? He was careful not to bring this up again.

The island man fumbled with something, hung the flashlight on a nail, and said, "Later you turn it off."

The room was smaller than it looked from the outside and hangers with ragged clothes covered the walls.

Before leaving, he warned him that he was an early riser and that he did not have to have breakfast with him.

From the small window came some quiet coolness; the insects just barely snored, or maybe it was the moon. Before turning off the flashlight, the railroad man noticed that the island man had forgotten his binoculars and hurried out, but he saw no one.

By dawn, he was already awake and had been standing outside for a while, sitting on the wood, appearing to be waiting for Chicú, the owner. Instead Carlo arrived. "It's me," he said from the bottom of the terrace. From his bag, he pulled out a clean, ironed shirt, a sweater, an undershirt. The railroad man tried everything on and then they had breakfast. The tomatoes were leftovers from the night before and the island man pulled other things out of the bag: a paper bag with two pieces of focaccia, sketch paper, pencils, and another bag.

When they stood up and the railroad man slung his bag over his shoulder, reluctantly throwing some clothing onto the trash pile, the island man handed him the second bag as well. "Try them on, they are comfortable."

A pair of leather sandals. After trying them on, the railroad man left them on and slipped his boots into his backpack, which had never been this full.

"You forgot your binoculars yesterday."

The island man wandered around a bit, looking at where they had eaten dinner and breakfast. "Where did I leave them?"

"Inside, on the table." He went in to get them for him, and the island man thanked him, and shrugged. "I don't need them today anyway; it wasn't there at sunrise, and when it's like this, it's not there at sunset either."

"Maybe…but didn't you say that you can always see it from Alassio?"

"I said often."

The railroad man said nothing. He moved his feet in his sandals, looking at them; they were very comfortable.

"Yesterday I told you about my animals."

The railroad man took a dozen crumpled sheets of paper from the island man's hands. There were drawings of mice, owls, crows, turtles, lizards, flies, snakes, a whale, a dog–some even on the same sheet. They were almost all in pencil, though some were colored or partly colored, and a couple were merely quick sketches; you couldn't even tell what animals they were, but they were animals. The railroad man stared at some of them longer than others, comparing them to each other as if they were islands.

"Which one do you want? I'll give you one."

"The lizards." He counted them; there were two, one of which was just the little head of a lizard.

"It's not just any lizard, it's the ocellated lizard. You rarely ever see it, it's big–a beast like this–and it has a back as blue as the sea." The island man had to specify all these details because the lizards were in pencil, and it was not clear how big and different they were from a normal lizard.

"Maybe you've seen it along the railroads, in the crevices?"

"If I had seen a blue-headed lizard, I would have remembered it...."

"Not the head, the back."

"And have you seen it?"

"No, but a friend told me about it...." He breathed as if he wanted to tell him a long story, and looked at the sea beyond the shack. But then, he said just a few words. "As a child, this friend met a great man who, before he took his life, had had an obsession, like you with the tracks and I with the islands and carob trees. His was the ocellated lizard."

The railroad man let him talk while he listed his beasts; he always found beasts lying dead on the tracks—badgers that had dried up days ago, foxes, even a wild boar. On summer nights, they would fall asleep on the cool iron of the tracks and the train would surprise the life out of them. Some were already rotten when he found them. He could hear them from afar, their hides drained, coming off, bitten by other animals, and by now full of worms, or only the bones remained.

At the end of the terraced olive groves, they walked downhill, not on the road from the day before. Carlo, who knew the shortcuts, lead the way down steps with flower pots and, every so often, they had to stop and sidestep, encountering bathers with inflatable floats and rafts, oars.

When they reached a bottleneck in the flatland, Carlo, or the island man, suddenly turned around and handed him the binoculars and a couple of bills. He did not have to insist much. Finally, the railroad man put the money in his pocket, opened the case, took a good look at that object that was now his, and gently slipped it into his backpack.

In front of the tracks, they parted without hardly saying anything more to each other. The island man took the underpass and the railroad man followed with his eyes that slightly pendulous step—somewhat like his own—accustomed to the coarse-grained gravel.

He walked among the rubbish and broken bottles until he sat on a concrete power box, and instead of sandals—they were not ideal along the tracks—he wore boots.

He thought about how many times he had seen lizards escape, balancing on the tracks, but never such a reptile, with its opened throat and blue back.

He crouched down on the tracks to feel their heat and remember the first time, in Sanremo. It was cold then. Then, he did something he never did: he climbed the platform and balanced himself on it, his hand on his forehead to shield himself from the sun, and from up there, from that slight elevation, he looked down at the streets, toward the sea, appearing to have discovered Carlo's dangling step.

When he got hungry, beyond Alassio, well after the railroad had returned to being encased by walls, barbed wire, and agaves, he stopped and pulled out the tomatoes. They were soft and he ate them with the last piece of focaccia. Inside his backpack, his fingers were surprised to recognize the cylindrical shape of the binocular case.

Evening caught him before he reached Albenga, so he looked for a quiet place. It was not an amazing place, but he still thought he would stay there for a few days, or more, maybe a month; he never knew the length of his stops. That was why, in so many years, his road map had made much less progress than it should have, and he blamed himself for some of these delays and stops.

Before it got dark, he put his hands in his backpack again. He opened up his binoculars as the island man had taught him, and moved them through the network of narrow streets that died on the shoreline, and inland, where glass greenhouses sparkled. He waited until evening finally invaded the plaster and car headlights crossed. It was too early for fireflies.

Albenga was an expanse of land, the largest plain he ever saw on his way; it gave a feeling of easy living. Then, at the bottom, other mountains began, and in the whiteness, the thin trunks of the pines stood out.

Apart from the obvious things—the sandals, the binoculars, the lizard drawings, and another couple of crumpled sheets of floating islands—it was as if, come evening, the island man had left no other traces of himself. Only the islet, there in front of him, with vague outlines, and his mind traced the head and neck of a snake and the hump of a camel, as he had seen it earlier that day and the day before. It had been the island of Alassio and now it was the island of Albenga, and even today, it stood in the water, ready to enter the past.

ITALO AND CARLO

The man who got off the train with the light luggage is Italo Calvino. Waiting for him is Carlo, the sketcher of islands. Italo calls him by his last name and they greet each other affectionately. They don't meet often and when they do, Italo prefers to take his car, but this time he was in Sanremo on his way to Turin, or maybe it's the other way around; from Turin, the train was taking him to Sanremo, and Alassio seemed to him a pleasant stop.

They leave the station–there are no cars waiting to go up to the villa– and after the Via Aurelia, the zig-zag of the mule path to Solva awaits them. Calvino knows all the tricks to cut the climb in half, but not those to reduce fatigue, and Carlo has also been frequenting Liguria for years now. He is an accomplished painter and has done a few portraits of Calvino, but they usually talk about books because Carlo is Carlo Levi and he is an Einaudi author, the publishing house Calvino works for.

They stop to catch their breath in front of the sea. It is afternoon and Corsica could appear today; it's September and the air is shiny. "At dawn, it was there," says Carlo Levi. An impression of Corsica, with its unchanged weather conditions, is already more than promised. But at sunset, Italo Calvino will be back on his train.

The sea begins a little further down, beyond the slope of pines and roofs, and rises as if driven by an opposite, hidden wave.

Calvino's eyes often encountered these effects and these descending worlds, with their liquid counterpart rising to the horizon. Obstacles too: covering the expanse of diamonds are three or four gigantic pines, which in prose could amount to a series of em dashes; in one em dash, a frond shifts, allowing the eye to see what follows in the distance.

They cannot see the railroad; it is neither beyond the incision nor west or east. But it is what they will talk about today. Because today, Carlo Levi tells him what happened to him a few weeks earlier at the beach.

"I met him. He passed through here, I even took some photos of him."

"Who are you talking about?"

"A long time ago, you told me, you were a little boy and you met Benjamin, who told you that he was looking for the giant lizard. Even I started drawing it because of how much you talked about it...and you had told Benjamin the story of the railroad boy...." Calvino remembers telling him those things from before the war, things from the days even before the creation of the National Union of Anti-Aircraft Protection. He is interested in hearing more, as if, without knowing it, he came for that purpose.

"He's not a child anymore, Calvino, but he's just as you described him, just as you told Benjamin. He started chasing railroads as a child."

Italo Calvino would gladly move the foliage to see only the sea. He says nothing.

"He was practicing swimming, Calvino; we were at the Coscia Tower."

Italo Calvino tries to smile but fails. "Did he have it written on his forehead that it was him?"

Carlo Levi explains to him how things went.

"You know, he knows there is someone—he knows about you—who wanted to write his story. He's read it; a childhood friend of yours mentioned it in some article. He reads, he stops in libraries to escape the cold...then he leaves again."

"And in what direction did he go?"

"East, always east. At this point, he must be just after Albenga. He doesn't go fast, and he stops happily along the escarpments; if it doesn't rain, he sunbathes on the rocks and in the summer he swims. He works where he can and he stops for months, even a year, where he pleases. Now he must be looking for the lizard. It has always fascinated me since you told me about it and you could tell that it fascinated him, too. When I asked him to choose between the drawings, he did not hesitate and chose the two drawings of the lizard...."

"In that case, it's literary instigation." Now, they laugh.

Then Calvino gets serious again. "You mentioned photos."

"At least three."

"What is it?"

"It's just that not a single one came out, they're all blank...he doesn't exist, he's just a literary character invented by you, and because of that, he erases every picture of himself and every background behind him."

"Oh, stop it...it's no use walking around with a big camera like that if you don't know how to use it."

There are two little girls in the park, one must be the daughter of the man who takes care of the hedges around the house, playing with a few things and not caring about the two gentlemen laughing and looking at the sea and the hills. There is nothing strange about that afternoon in the park. Occasionally, the roar of a train sounds above, not interrupting their conversations and laughter, but their conversations often stop for no reason. Italo is a silent man, and today he has indulged in far too much railroad verbiage. He no longer feels like laughing, but he knows, however, that he must come to terms with this parallel story of his that seeks him out, so he tries to laugh.

And now that Carlo Levi tells him that he has met this man and that this man walks there, in front of them, Italo Calvino hears his railroad steps from afar. He will write many more stories, yet the story of the boy and his dream, of his now immense obsession as an adult, he will be unable to tell. It would require a long line, just barely curving, every now and then, according to the Ligurian railroad, with its stations, its freight terminals...the impossible horizontal Liguria. An arrogant matter.

"You know Carlo, I've spent years, my entire life, every day, writing to writers, most of the time to strangers, telling them, 'I've read your manuscript, I've read, *your* manuscript.' Thousands of letters...it was as if every time I denied myself to him, to the desire to write to him and tell him who I am, to tell him who he is, to say, 'I know you.' And to have him tell me what life looks like from a crosstie that becomes precedent to the future crosstie that becomes the present, and the present as a gesture and space of the suspended step. I don't know if that's it. I can only imagine, but he knows. Do I also step from one word to another?"

They can't laugh right away, but then they do, and the little girls turn to look at them.

AFTER ALBENGA

Summer was short-lived, with winter came sparkling days that were still quite warm, though they flew by. Sometimes he would lie for hours, hidden among the tepid stones, pointing his binoculars between each wrinkle. The ocellated lizard would not appear. He even doubted its existence, were it not for that pair of drawings and the information he gathered in the Spotorno library that claimed that that type of saurian lived happily in Liguria, especially around Pompeiana, and fed on insects and ripe fruit.

Along the railroad, he would unfold the paper to compare the drawn head with that of ordinary lizards. If it was windy, he would put the big rusty bolt on top of it. He was never separated from it again. He would not part with anything. Or at night, he would compare the drawing of the head with the stern glare and mouth of geckos. He would look for them on the crusts of the plaster, on the tracks, on the few square meters of the grassy field.

His mother once warned him that they were poisonous animals. He still obeyed her to this day, though he did not think this was entirely true. They were as mild as a railroad walker can be.

He stood there, occasionally pointing his binoculars farther away, looking for workers in the fields. The mowers, with their tics, a constant motion of open arms, and the scythe cutting the grass in waves. In the gardens populated by day by curved men and children and women, there were those who barely popped out of the arches made by the oxheart tomatoes, those who irrigated, those who harvested, those who wore strange metal backpacks and scattered blue spit into the air around the fruit trees. Then the night would pass him by. By now, he was an expert; from afar, he could point out oranges and persimmons, his favorite winter fruit. He would lower the branches and strip the plant bare, leaving only one fruit because Carlo had explained to him that a plant needs fruit to feed itself slowly during the rest of the season. It was a nice gesture, and he thought he had become a man of nice gestures.

Sooner or later, he stopped at Cape Lena and on a stone, he drew Gallinara, which he could see far to the east. As if to practice, he had seen the architecture of Corsica elsewhere, with its broken coastlines, realizing that after all, observed through binoculars, yes, it was always the same island, but on paper, it was not because he could not draw it the same as the others. And sometimes he was nostalgic for that island man Carlo.

He liked the moment when his eyes first discovered the obstacle between the railroad and the horizon, between the railroad and, toward the east, Cape Noli, ready to break away from the world, at any moment, and to get lost mottling the water for a while with edges, trimmings, and streaks the color of the earth.

Then came the day when he happened to be in front of an island he had never seen—a real island—and there, too, he decided to stop for a long time, as if he were waiting for someone.

His stay in Spotorno, the town before the island and Torre del Mare, would undoubtedly be his longest stay in one place. Almost a year.

After the station, the tracks rammed through a seemingly small tunnel, a more gray and deserted entrance than usual; lower than usual too, it seemed almost impossible for a train to pass through there. He entered it because it was raining, and did not continue inside it. Once the bad weather ended, he returned to the station and then, through the underpass and alleys, almost ended up in the sea.

He felt a bit like he was on vacation that day, for no reason, perhaps just because it was that time of year: during the day, the sun had enough time to dry the gravel and dampness of the alleys, and he liked the long evenings of Spotorno.

In Torre del Mare, between Spotorno and Bergeggi, while wandering around the pine forests, he met a gentleman from Milan, wealthy in his own right and a translator. He had never met a translator before and started asking him a lot of questions about his business. For example, what was the point of wasting his days manipulating other people's things, from one language to another, at the expense of his life. The translator laughed it off and told him that it was like walking down the tracks for him; it wasn't like anyone had forced him to, it had to be some kind of plan. Looking for a ball had probably become a good excuse.

"No, it's not like that, " said the railroad man.

"Bullshit," said the translator. It is like that.

This upset him. For him, there was more at stake, the fictional aspect of the Sanremo writer, and the fact that just as one could tamper with the meaning and idea of another person and translate it, so could one tamper with another's destiny. The Milanese translator—he must have been familiar with Calvino's work—chuckled, "Come on."

He had returned from the shelves of the well-stocked bookcase (they were having tea in the living room of his house, in front of the sea) with a book by Calvino, the latest, *Mr. Palomar*, and read a few lines from it.

Reading a wave.

The sea is barely wrinkled, and little waves strike the sandy shore. Mr. Palomar is standing on the shore, looking at a wave. Not that he is lost in contemplation of the waves. He is not lost, because he is quite aware of what he is doing: he wants to look at a wave and he is looking at it.

The railroad man felt upset once again. He had missed it, how was it possible— in Albenga, he had not found any new Calvino, not even in Finale Ligure. The Milanese translator had already read it and gave it to him as a gift. He prepared some pasta with sauce and in the end, offered him shelter. There was a dry and clean basement, with a cot, a bathroom, even an electric heater. The railroad man accepted, although he would have preferred to go back to the railroad because he did not like to let go.

"Come on, let go of the tracks? Bullshit," said the translator.

Early in the morning, after breakfast, the railroad man seriously expressed his intention to leave. The translator wanted to accompany him in the car, so they went up to the garage, which was on the roof of the cottage and overlooked the street, but the railroad man, at the cost of telling him many lies again, said he could not accept and would go on foot—he had never been in a car, only on a bus, as a child with his mother—and pointed west, as he did every time he talked about his past.

From the sides of the roof, the sea poked through the foliage. The clean smell of pine was harsh and strong. Spotorno stretched just into the distance, and in front of Torre del Mare floated the island of Bergeggi in the sun.

He asked him if he had ever been there, and the translator said yes, as a boy, he had gone there a couple of times by boat with friends. He made a gesture as if to indicate his past as well. He used to go to Torre del Mare every year–in reality, he used to go there for the sea–but now he did not go there anymore to swim. He preferred to read the waves through the exercise of Mr. Palomar and others. He said this in a tone as if he were writing something at that moment, and the railroad man made a sound with his nose.

Below the cottage, the property descended a few terraces. The railroad man leaned over and the translator pointed out to him all the work that needed to be done. If he could do the walls, there was work for him. He said no, walls he couldn't do, but strength work (that's exactly what he said), like moving stones and digging a threshold, yes. Well, said the translator, there were stones to be recovered under the landslide, if his railroad walks could wait and he felt like working. There was also the carpet of leaves and pine needles to rake and take to the dumpsters.

The railroad man accepted and began right away. He gladly toiled in the dirt, especially if he didn't have to enter pesticide-ridden greenhouses. The translator treated him well; every couple of hours, he would call him over to have a glass of wine or a soda, and they would stand for a while on the terrace looking at the blue void between the foliage, and then he was the one who had to say, "Well, I'm going back to the stones, otherwise we'll eat everything here," or "He who looks at the sea from the fields turns around and there is still work to be done." The latter he had heard from the farmers.

In the evening, the work was practically done and the railroad man was paid handsomely. He stayed for dinner, but he ate much less than at lunch: just a little soup and a piece of gruyere cheese, with a glass of lambrusco, his favorite wine.

After dinner, they put on their jackets and stayed on the terrace for a long time, talking about the fact that that afternoon, they had forgotten to watch the wave, the single wave of Mr. Palomar.

The railroad man ended up sleeping in the basement that night as well. The translator had already explained to him how to turn the electric heater on and off, but he didn't need to. These electric things, the railroad man said, intimidated him, and besides, it had been too hot the other night as well.

He placed *Mr. Palomar* next to the bed and went to brush his teeth for a long time—he rarely managed to do so. Once in bed, he began the tale of the bare breasts, but did not finish it and got up to turn off the light because he became sleepy almost immediately.

After a while, he heard a knock.

"Come in," he said. The door was not locked, and, for that matter, on second thought, he had never locked a door in his life.

The translator turned on the light; he was holding a pair of glasses.

"Can you see well? They're for reading."

The railroad man tried the glasses on a few lines of *Mr. Palomar*'s bare breasts. A miracle—as he went along, he felt a growing nostalgia for the younger days when he read in the libraries of Diano and San Bartolomeo.

"So, how are they?"

"They make me nostalgic," he said.

"Well, that's no good…shall I turn off the light?"

"No, I'm going to read some more… let's see what Mr. Palomar is up to."

Calvino's Stations

If there was one thing in all those years that he had lost along the way, it was a sense of time, and somehow Calvino's books had made up for it. One after another, they provided some chronological order to his railroad existence. He could not remember the release of an old novel like *The Path to the Nest of Spiders*; it spoke of its prehistory, having come out in 1947, when Italo was twenty-four years old, and he did not yet frequent libraries. But one day, in Diano or San Bartolomeo, he had discovered those special places full of book stores and by chance, his eyes had fallen on *The Argentine Ant* and then on the tales of *The Crow Comes Last*. A miracle, he let out a long gasp, rereading and recognizing landscapes, faces, tics, and dialogues he heard from the Italian partisans. Later he had found that famous article by Duilio Cossu, and then it was as if the words of his story, the adventure and something of his own, yet unknown, had been skewered by the harpoon of literature, by the miracle of literature.

Calvino wrote one book a year, moving easily from novels to essays, directing series, and he waited for his books as one waits for the train at a new station. He would ask the librarians; for example, in Alassio, they would say, "Not yet, *Italian Folktales* will be out in three months," and he would count on it and find the *Folktales* in Loano or Pietra. And so on and so forth.

And so the years passed and the books and his life could be said to have known a single frontier, a real watershed. It had happened where *Mr. Palomar* takes place, precisely there, in Torre del Mare, on the day he had received reading glasses as a gift. For him, they had meant entry into achieved seniority. Not a decadence. Or perhaps the beginning, rather, of a decadence, something intuitable through the awareness that he could no longer see the world as he had seen it before.

It had started raining again. In the evenings, he found shelter under a portico, among the pallets of a construction site, and for his walks around town, he bought an umbrella. Driven by poverty, one day he walked the entire seaside, then went up toward the pine forests and back to the translator's house. He feared he had returned to Milan, where he lived during the winter, but instead, he was still in Torre del Mare finishing the translation of the *Gypsy Ballads*. He was going away at the end of the month, he said, and in the meantime, he would host him if he wanted, and would gladly offer him a bowl of soup and whatever else was available.

The last couple of days, the weather cleared up and the translator offered him another little job in his cousin's garden.

He did not start early in the morning. First, he would walk along the beach and stand there a few hours, watching the wave of Mr. Palomar, as if he were waiting for spring. Then, he would have lunch with the translator at the local Italian restaurant, and in the afternoon, he would walk up the ridge of the pine forests, go down into the garden, arm himself with a spike, and spit on his palms as he remembered seeing the farmers do in the terraces above Sanremo. He would dig thresholds for new walls and pile up stones, dividing the small from the large, the good from the bad, to use for drainage. The usual things: he carried bags of cement and sandstone in buckets that the truck unloaded at the entrance to the roof. Basically, he would prepare everything for when the mason would come to raise the wall. Every once in a while, a gecko would awake from hibernation, surprised and dry between the stones, and he would watch it closely as it yawned—half dead and cold— and rescue it.

He still thought about the ocellated lizard, but less so. He would work until a certain time, usually until the sea grew greyer than the sky, and the translator would come out on the terrace and tell him that was enough for today because it was about to become humid, and he had never killed anyone to deserve that kind of punishment. Then the railroad man would straighten his back, look at the job done, and feel satisfied.

It was during those evenings that he discovered the works of Camillo Sbarbaro—the translator always talked about him about at dinner. From one of the borrowed books in the house, he wrote down Sbarbaro's poem to his father, and before he fell asleep, he read it—the miraculous glasses on his nose—and knew it by heart.

Father, even if you weren't my father,
were you an utter stranger,
for your own self I'd love you.

He had almost never had a father. He only remembered a mother, and he accepted it all, all except one thing he had never come to terms with: the child who played ball in the alleys had not even known his grandparents. How was it possible that his mother had never told him about them? Wouldn't that be like suffering an amputation? Not knowing where all those grandparents had been during their lives, whether they had lived in Sanremo or in another city...and the writer who had invented the words of his life, he too, how could he have forgotten such a thing?

And in all that time, in all those years of moving eastward, of winter stays and nights, of fierce, incandescent summer light that covered his skin with blisters, his writer had never stopped writing and he had never stopped reading him. He liked him very much now. You know these pages well now, he told himself, although sometimes this Calvino ended up having too many expectations for his books and some books had literally ended up disappointing him a bit. *The Baron in the Trees,* so long ago, on the other hand, had not disappointed him at all; it had seemed wonderful to him, a kind of aerial alter ego of his own. Was that who he was? A living being who spent the rest of his days among the plants as he had decided to live on railroads. The world seen from an altitude, no matter which, in solitude? *You suffer from vertigo, that's why he made you keep your feet on the ground.* Was his writer a loner, too? But what was he writing certain books like *Collection of Sand* for when someone like him, clearly full of imagination, could write who knows what other adventures of ants and nonexistent knights? Every year, he waited for the new book to come out; at the library, they would tell him, "Almost, just a little longer," and at the right moment, he would pass by the bookstore and find the new book, immediately read a few pages standing there, and look forward to finding it in the library. Then he would sit comfortably at a large table, pull his glasses out of his breast pocket, and sigh.

It cannot be said that Italo returns to Sanremo often. Does a man as accustomed as he is to classifying every item, as well as to literature, extend the same rigor to life? Surely he must be wondering what will become of Villa Meridiana and the plethora of documents, essays, monographs, books, and annotations that his parents gathered between stays in Mexico, Cuba, and Sanremo. He must have an idea, but when his father died, did he discuss this with his brother Floriano and his mother?

Sometimes when he returns, he finds his mother among the irises, her favorite flowers. At this point, he is an important writer, but before her, somehow, there is still a child, an Italo who read and preferred the movie theater and the sea to the countryside and botany.

The story of the little boy—now the man—on the railroads chased the writer and filled some of his stories with railroads, but one thing he would have never expected was that someday his mother would tell him about it as well.

"Last month, a lady passed through here, as if by chance, but then she admitted that she came on purpose. She wanted to talk to you, not give you things to read," she says quickly. "She wanted to talk about her son who left home many years ago...."

Italo raises his eyebrow again, looking for the sea. Something is troubling him, as when long ago, his friend Duilio, and Carlo Levi, revealed the same things to him. But now it is his mother talking to him and he would like to change the subject.

"Don't worry. Why should you worry? She just wanted to tell me how things were for her; since her son left as a child, life ended for her. She told me that according to the *carabinieri*, who spoke with one of his friends, he chased the tracks, but she doesn't think so, she thinks he simply left, who knows where to, many years ago, before the war...what kind of a child leaves like that?"

"Was he a normal child? He would be my age...."

"More or less, yes, he was a child, before the war...and now he's a middle-aged man...and who knows where he is, maybe he stopped somewhere...but he never came back, that's for sure." She spreads her arms out a little and shrugs.

"You know why she came to see you? Because when I was a kid, I had told Walter Benjamin about this. Remember, I had run into him? I never told you anything about the fable of the child who goes searching for the end of the tracks, but Benjamin, yes...then I had told Duilio about it, and I would have never thought it would become an obsession for a child, who on his own...his mother therefore came to you because there is this rumor going around...but it's like if a woman goes to another woman and says you know, my son is your son's son...right?"

"What are you talking about? It's not...if I had known this would upset you, I wouldn't have told you anything. In reality, she is not looking for you or to tell you, she just wanted to meet me."

"The mother of the child who invented her son's fate—does she still hope to find him?"

His mother shakes her head no.

ARENZANO STATION

Before Arenzano, the railroad went through a series of tunnels and this time, it was impossible to disregard them because the cliffs pierced by the tunnels rose vertically and then descended again on the other side that overlooked the cliffs and the sea. Bends of sand and gravel, with a few *gozzi*[5] on the beach, alternated on the cliffs, and in the summer–he arrived with the first heat of the season–bathers placed deck chairs and umbrellas there.

He slept there the first night; he waited for everyone to leave, took his last swim with the moon, then dried off and found shelter under one of the *gozzi*.

It was not the first time he slept under one; the shoreline was full of them, the little boats of fishermen and sea enthusiasts, turned over on their bellies, some placed on four logs that one could slip under without even having to lift them up. He would stay there until the first light penetrated his sleep along with the cry of the seagulls, which brought a nice smell of seaweed. He would stay curled up a little longer, thinking about that sly Mr. Palomar out there, intent on calculating the intervals between waves.

On the first morning–the idea was to stay there a few days–when he came out, it was cloudy and no one was there yet. Better this way. He looked up at the cliff carved obliquely by a stone staircase. He would have liked to climb it, get up to the top and see the bay and what was hiding at sea, but first he went to pee in a corner and stretch his back, and in the meantime, had discarded the thought of the scenic view. In the past, he would not have thought twice about it, but now he knew full well that climbs, the stairs, and the heat wore him out immediately. He undressed, stepped into the clear water, felt like urinating again, and this time, did so in the sea. If he stayed a little longer in the water, it was to postpone the effort of getting out; he hated fac-

---

[5] A traditional wooden boat that was originally used for fishing and is now commonly used for cruising.

ing the pebble beach barefoot. He had sore feet, and the seawater managed to soothe them, but it could do nothing against his abrasions and inflamed heels. They were the ankles of an old soccer player.

Arenzano began beyond the entrance of the tunnel to the east. One small road led into the town and another conveniently descended from the plateau and pine forest. When he looked up there again, he regretted not having gone up to get a view of the town and the bay, but if he stayed a few days—he felt the need to rest his bones, bathe in the water— sooner or later, he could indulge in a nice exploration of the plateau through the convenient access.

In fact, he never knew if once he arrived in a place he would settle there for a while, just as he did not know why he liked certain places rather than others. Arenzano, however, he chose because, not far from the station, he found a park with benches, paths, and flower beds inhabited by a few rabbits and an all-blue peacock. He liked it right away and that day, he could not stop laughing.

Until a certain time, it was a park frequented by mothers and children on bikes that splashed the gravel, but the peacock was unintimidated.

Every time, a while after a train passed by (only the local ones, intercity trains did not stop there), passengers would appear at the park entrance. They usually chose Arenzano for its bathing establishments and, with their backpacks or suitcases, they stopped to rest. They would sit on the benches by the gate, looking at the sea at the bottom of the slope, and after a while, the peacock would arrive. When they left Arenzano, before catching the train, they would sit on the benches again, as if to bid farewell to their vacation, and after a while, the peacock would arrive.

One day, it was a very beautiful lady's turn; with her backpack on her shoulders, the peacock approached her. The railroad man, lying on one of the benches outside, was dozing off. The lady pulled out a foil, and upon hearing the sound of bites of watermelon, the railroad man opened his eyes.

"I'm sorry I woke you up," said the lady. She knew how to make it up to him and handed him a piece.

"Do I need to give him some too?" She had very white teeth and round calves, massacred by mosquitoes, but nonetheless very beautiful and tan.

He quickly got up and returned to his bench with the watermelon slice, immediately took a good bite, and said it was good and he would like to repay her.

She acted as if she had not heard him, and gave a piece of watermelon to the peacock as well, who pecked it just as eagerly.

"Are you going to the beach?"

"If I can find a spot."

"The water is clean and warm, I took a swim this morning...you know, I've been here for almost a month and in the morning, I go down, take a swim in the public beach, and then walk to the railroad or go up to the pine forest...." And he moved his hand to the west, as he did to indicate the past. She said nothing, and before lying down again, he added, "When the heat haunts me, I come back here."

"Do you do anything else?"

Stretched out, he says, "I cleaned vegetable gardens, but that was before the heat, when the sun didn't burn as much. They told me to come back in the fall, but who knows if I'll still be here in the fall–can you swim?"

"Sort of, where my feet can touch the bottom."

"Here's how I'll pay you back. We'll eat a sandwich and another half a watermelon and in return, I'll teach you how to swim. I'll hold you like this...." He got up again and stretched out his hands and arms as if to hold her horizontally. "I'll hold you and you'll kick."

"Give it up," she said as if he had tickled her belly.

She was truly beautiful. The skin above her lip was covered in sweat and she had such white teeth that he was ashamed to smile. When she left him with the last slice of watermelon, he thanked her with a half bow, ate a piece immediately, and saved the rest for later. He stretched back on the planks and smiled for a while. *Maybe she's taken*, he told himself. Almost immediately, he ate the rest of the watermelon in smooth motions, so that he did not interrupt his bite but absorbed every juice and then spit out the seeds.

She's probably taken, he answered himself. The peacock circled him. He laid the rind on the ground, a little further away, for it to peck at, but the peacock paid it no mind and went back to him.

"Give it up," he said. "That's all I have."

One of those days spent in the Arenzano park (before the policemen one morning asked him for his documents and suggested he find another place), he woke up in his bed of cardboard and rags at the edge of the park, and remembered the dream he had just had. He had arrived in Camogli, after so much travel and so much hunger, and had stopped because the railroad ended there. However, if he thought about the journey in the dream, along with the hunger and other things that had happened, he did not remember going through Genoa. How was this possible? Genoa, with its many stations that all the vagabonds talked about, its forest of tracks and bricks…if Savona and Albenga had already been a kind of labyrinth….

At some point, however, he began to cross Genoa, station after station; first Voltri, then Sestri Ponente, with its bridge and airport signs, and tunnels full of pipes and power lines, a tangle that inexorably introduced Sampierdarena and then Principe. Faced with the sight of the twenty or so railroads in Principe, including a couple underground, he decided to take a longer route so as not to run the risk of having to cross any of them. He found himself at the edge of the immense clearing of Brignole, with its classification yard and little stations.

From there on, more islands would emerge sooner or later, he expected, for he had already drawn them.

The Gulf islands, the Federici islands (he had transcribed the names from atlases), Palmaria, the first one past Quarto and Quinto, Nervi, Rapallo, along the Riviera dei Giardini, so much less beautiful than the Riviera degli Orti, which he had learned about in his youth.

What about that Carlo of the drawings? He always thought of him, as one thinks of a real person who, in the same breath, perhaps never existed, infinitely distant in time. The drawings he had received as a gift he no longer owned, flown away after forgetting to place a bolt or a small rock on them. The binoculars had broken and he had kept them for a while, until he got rid of them, or lost them. Like time. How far away Alassio was.

THE MOTHER AND THE LETTERS

When his mother died on March 31, 1978 in Sanremo, Calvino knew he had no one left there. Born in Sassari, his mother was a famous botanist.

Not even property will tie Calvino to the city anymore. Is there a desire in him to live elsewhere, to buy a house in Rome? Rome, Paris, New York. He likes big cities, and Sanremo has turned into a kind of concrete archaeological site. The bizarre characters, old noblemen or fallen noblemen; just a human decadence endures. But these are things that can only populate pages.

After the funeral, in those early days of April, Calvino stayed a few days at Villa Meridiana; or rather, left and returned.

He stands in front of the large window, knowing it will not be long before he leaves his descending world, and turns to lay a hand on certain desks, the book shelves, the drawers that hold prehistory. Is Floriano, the other brother who disregarded his parents' dreams, gone? He will briefly return to meet him and discuss the future of Villa Meridiana with him. He is certainly not there at the moment, not in the studio. Nor is Libereso there anymore—not that day, at least—but Italo can picture him among the plants, recognize his curly head that moved like a cloud in the green, among the barks, beyond the glass. They decided long ago to donate the entire library to the municipality. Or is this a new idea, something that matured after her death? At first they will try to sell the villa to the municipality—the whole property, the swaths of land, the exotic plants, the greenhouses, one conglomeration, the Calvino conglomeration. And they won't succeed. But right now Calvino doesn't know and doesn't think about it. So what does he think about? The papers—what else—the dozens of drafts of his manuscripts, the drafts of his letters. "I've read," is how all his letters start…right, how many people must he have written to whose work he claimed to have read. "I've read"…if he thinks about this, it's like thinking about the things he didn't write…about a child on the railroad, about Benjamin's ocellated lizard? Does it really exist? In so many months in the mountains he never saw it; sometimes he came down almost on purpose, armed and sent there to participate in some light action, and stopped above Bajardo, consuming his spare time looking for its figure surprised by the moonlight, and if he was on guard during the day and it buried itself in the cracks, his eye would be lost in the blue reflections of the cysts, in the waves of the heathers, in the blooming gorse, and his ear would delude itself into catching the rustle of a reptile.

"I was in San Giovanni, last year, but I never met you...maybe you've already seen the ocellated lizard."

"Do you know it? My father found a skeleton of one, a beast like this."

"You're exaggerating."

"I swear. So you know it...."

"Let's just say I look for it."

"It never shows itself."

"I'm afraid not."

He opens a drawer—he knows where to look, a man accustomed to sorting. Everything is inside one pale blue folder. Exactly thirty-three years have passed.

One of the sheets at the bottom bears the date.

Imperia 10/27/1945

In witness whereof.

But there is no signature.

Duties performed within the Thirtieth Formation.

Armed actions in which he took part during the aforementioned period:

Baiardo (March).

Other possible services.

No response.

Did you sustain any injuries as a result of your partisan activity?

No response.

Were you in prison or a concentration camp for partisan activity?

Yes, caught in the San Romolo roundup; enlisted in the republic of Salò, arrested for three days in Santa Tecla.

Partisan rank:

Garibaldino

Names of commanders and comrades who can testify about what is stated in this form:

Umberto, Leone, Riccardo, Battagliero, Olmo.

I pledge not to join other similar partisan formations.

In witness whereof.

He puts it down. On the other form written in capital letters is:

NATIONAL ASSOCIATION OF ITALIAN PARTISANS

Section of Sanremo (63)

Application for admission

The undersigned requests admission to the Partisan Association of Imperia and for this purpose provides the following biographical data, which he on his honor declares to be true:

Last name and first name Calvino Italo

Battle name Santiago

Place of birth Santiago de las Vegas

Province Cuba

Date of birth 10/15/1923

Nationality Italian

Father Mario

Mother Mameli Eva

Current Address Villa Meridiana Sanremo

Profession Student

Schools attended high school specializing in classical studies and agricultural college

Military service after September 8, 1943

Military branch sedentari[6]

COMMITTEE OF NATIONAL LIBERATION FOR NORTH ITALY

Sanremo District

NO. 6033 Protocol

Statement

It is stated that Calvino Italo di Mario born in Santiago de las

---

[6] This was a military branch that existed in Fascist Italy and involved administrative work for the government.

Vegas on 10/15/23 was a part of the Matteotti citizen brigade, Le-one Detachment.

In a document titled PERSONAL NOTES they had misstated his birthplace:

Born in Santiago Province of Chile

Familial status Single

Economic status Good

The rest are demobilization forms with general questions that were unanswered:

Arrested by the Nazi-fascists?

Date, location.

Release dates.

Or evasion dates.

Fallen? (in combat, shot, as a result of wounds, due to illness)

His eyes fall on a less yellowed letter, sent by the publishing house only two years earlier. Typewritten.

Giulio Einaudi Publishing House

Turin April 8, 1976

Dear Amoretti,

It is with great pleasure that I receive your letter from April 3 and learn that the first volume of the *History of the Imperian Resistance* is about to be published. I thank you and all your comrades for inviting me to present this volume, together with the reprinting of the *Epic of the Barefoot Army*, a book on which I had collaborated.... Unfortunately, the invitation reached me too late. I have a prior commitment on that date....

Yours truly,

Italo Calvino

In pen:

If I had known in time about the reprinting of the *Epic of the Barefoot Army*, I would have pointed out to you a printing error: in the list of the partisans, my and my brother's last name appears as Caldino instead of Calvino. But perhaps since it was an anastatic reprint, there was no way to correct errors anyway.

PINE FORESTS AND DEATH

At one point, he had left the railroad. Paper and pencils at his disposal, he spent his afternoons drawing, getting rid of the drawings sooner or later, because he knew well that he could not carry everything in his backpack.

The islands (first the Palmaria family, and further south the Tino and Tinetto, joined together by three reefs, like three dots), the islands in general, and the encounter with Carlo; all those years left back there in the stations of a geographical time, had been in their own way a kind of watershed, like reading glasses. The end of youth and a strong body had coincided with the end of the Liguria of the Orti. Then, slowly, something had changed; there was no more rush (to arrive?) and that, too, perhaps depended on him. Right? Probably.

Having reached Camogli, long before Tino and Tinetto, he had recalled the strange dream of the end of the railroad he had in Arenzano. Everything emerged a bit, sooner or later, as if the churning waters of the seabed were clearing and the spear of enchantment found lived memories, figures and dreams.

He woke up shivering and often felt a strong force in his muscles, nerves, and blood, remembering the beautiful lady who had given him the watermelon. He hated himself because he had been incapable of saying anything to her except making that silly proposal to teach her how to swim, keeping her afloat. He stood there, thinking about her, massaging himself and feeling all the way to his guts, under his rags, in that chronic hunger for a woman, all his idiotic and miserly fate.

A truce. That's it. What was it that prevented him from taking a break, letting himself drift away, transported to some fertile valley? The thought of sleeping at night by a woman's side, in a clean bed, between sheets flooded by the moon? The unknown and risky condition of the abandonment of a railroad breath, in exchange for the silence of a stone village, with the swish of the stream under the bridges, he and the peace of another residence?

Until one day, by chance, one afternoon—after taking a refreshing dip in the creek pool, where he had been splashing around a lot lately—he had entered the library in Monterosso, the big town along whose stretch of railroad tracks he had long resided, and learned of his death, of Calvino's death, and by chance, since no one had taken the trouble of informing him that he had been dead for quite some time.

He learned about it in early summer; it was 1986, and the railroad man that day, despite his bathing, felt a great heat tread on his neck, like an anxious, clammy hand, but it is not true that at that moment he was thinking about sad things, much less about death; he never thought about anyone's death, let alone Calvino's. Perhaps one could say he was not thinking about death any more than he usually thought about it. That's all.

In Monterosso, and in the Cinque Terre in general, if he was not toiling as a laborer, he was more concerned with vertical figures, with a mineral landscape capable of reminding him of the Pigna, the historic center of his Sanremo.

Anyway, in one of the newspapers found in the reading room, he read that it was almost the first anniversary of his death, and then he sat at the table, exhausted. Had that much time passed? And had he, in all that time, gotten up in the morning and toiled as a laborer, or had he simply walked according to the universe's arrangements? In short, had he "gone going," critically observing every procedure, every code, without ever realizing what had happened, without ever knowing? That was how it had gone, it seems.

He died in Siena on September 19, 1985, and rested in a cemetery at the bottom of Tuscany.

And now that he was gone, how he would have wanted to meet him, now, to tell him, "I know who you are, you're Mr. Palomar, you're Marcovaldo, you're Pin, Cosimo…who are you?" And be asked the same. To know.

Calvino, the man who told his wife before he died that he felt his head burn like a lampshade.

He would have liked to arrive somewhere quickly. To walk to a cemetery gate, according to his self-imposed rules, his duty, of which he was grateful for, because for him, gratitude was indeed the most pleasant of duties. To stop there for a long time, as he did in important places, and sit in front of the grave all that time, his back against the trunk of a pine tree. The ultimate salute to his accomplice. A literary matter? Probably. He knew of no other: he had done it long ago in Spotorno at Camillo Sbarbaro's grave, the man who had managed to make him feel fatherless and grandfatherless, and then when he had stopped in Santa Margherita and touched the stones where the poet was born.

But now, Calvino had been dead for almost a year, and if he thought about it, if in that moment he got up from the Monterosso library table, and went down the stairs and exited the building, climbed over mounds and returned to his shiny tracks, he felt that for the first time in his life he could make the most sensible decision, and imagine, as he had always imagined, the possibility of a return home. Home? In any case, not go on anymore because if Calvino was dead, at the very least a contract was broken. Would he have revealed the ending of such a plot to the librarian, to the readers who stood there, in that early summer of 1986, begging as he did for a breath of air? Would he have confessed to them such an eventuality? The questions muddled his sense of direction; that's what they were for, he was his private *stempo*. Someone like him was not made of written words—the literary question was ridiculous—and his name, that's what mattered, no one had called him for years; his life without an identity card, his breath, they were his heart, bound to an infinite iron, bolted to the world, whose width stood in one hand exactly like a child's heart....

He immediately wanted to know more and asked the librarian to help him.

In his last few years, said the librarian, well-versed in the subject, the writer had written a lot. *If on a Winter's Night a Traveler, Cosmicomics,* and then, *Mr. Palomar—Mr. Palomar?* Come on, *Mr. Palomar* had come out two years before he died? But how was that possible? He had read it in Torre del Mare, as a guest of the translator, between Bergeggi and Spotorno...it was the translator himself who had given it to him as a gift, and it had been so long that he had managed to ruin it along the way and lose it, because the books in his backpack all faced the same fate.... So how was it possible, what was so frightening in the folds of his journey if the pages of a book that had come out only two or three years earlier brought him back to the remote Riviera degli Orti....

THE END OF LIGURIA

He did not leave immediately, and when he did, when he left Monterosso, he had saved some money. He had become specialized in painting railings, but on certain conditions; he asked his boss if he could use water-based paints because he was allergic to other products. And his boss bought him everything he needed; he was half his age and had a well-established business. The railroad man was going to leave the same day he learned of the writer's death, but his boss had begged him to stay; he had to delegate several jobs for houses occupied by tourists soon and he trusted him. So the railroad man stayed again that summer, and one evening in late September, after coming by to collect his pay, he said he was really leaving this time. His boss was sorry; he wanted to know why, whether it was a matter of money. He said no, it had never been a matter of money, it was just that when he had some change, he wanted to keep on going. That was all, and now he could get by for a bit.

Sometimes, during breaks, while eating a hot lunch in the local restaurant and watching the rain, or while they labored, his boss asked him to rest, to sit on the benches for a moment, saying that he was no longer a young man. The railroad man had tried to explain to him that lately, since he had learned of the death of a loved one, the torment of going forward to the east turned into the torment of wanting to return, as never before. And that worried him. His boss tilted his head to one side, looked at him as lizards do on tracks in the sun when they stare unsuspectingly at things. He did not understand and remembered that the railroad man once told him that he envied him. That night, before he left, they hugged, and the railroad man told him that he had never hugged a man. The little boss tilted his lizard head and lowered his gaze.

After leaving Monterosso behind, he found again for a few months the usual rotten tunnels (a doctor in the emergency room, alarmed by his breathing, had told him that sleeping in there was poison, but he shrugged his shoulders, as if to say come on, the paints on the other hand, those were poison), the articulated piers, the docks, the ship-yards, and a new landscape stinking of paint slowly immersed him in the city of La Spezia.

One day, from the railroad, he took an underpass, which was followed by wide lanes, and asked people where the library was. It was a well-stocked library, full of students, a whole school group, and the railroad man expressed his desire to check out everything they owned on Calvino. There must have been more than in Monterosso; in fact, he entered in the morning and left when it was dark.

Reports gathered in Monterosso were confirmed: on September 6 of last year, Italo Calvino was seized by a stroke. He was at his home in the Tuscan pine forest of Roccamare, preparing for his trip to the United States. Hospitalized first in the Misericordia Hospital in Grosseto, he was then transferred to Santa Maria della Scala Hospital in Siena, where he apparently regained consciousness and was awaiting an operation, but on Sept. 19, he died from a cerebral hemorrhage. He was buried in the garden cemetery of Castiglione della Pescaia, a place far from La Spezia. Indeed, the distance from La Spezia to Castiglione della Pescaia, he had noticed, was almost the same from Sanremo to La Spezia. On foot, it would have taken too long and with his precarious pace and joints, he never would have arrived. So he thought he could catch a train, perhaps switch trains somewhere, look for Castiglione della Pescaia—maybe a train would stop near the cemetery—and go to the garden cemetery, as he had done for Sbarbaro in Spotorno.

He hadn't looked for anything else in the library, not now. Just the trip's expected route by train, the stops, the distances, photos of the cemetery, things like that....

Going down the stairs of the building, pensively, he followed the smooth and spherical handrail like a railroad, and the streets brought him back to the suburbs, where he found the underpass, or maybe it was a different one, the tracks never ended.... What city was this, was it still La Spezia, what region was this?

Perhaps the place where he found himself, the escarpments and old stations, the shed with the broken roof that housed him for a few nights, had long since ceased to be the only possible universe, the only

Ligurian place containing the world, with the starry valleys, as narrow and long as the Milky Way, which he had learned to watch as if it were a small room, reading *Mr. Palomar*. In fact, from studying it in school, he remembered that to the right–to the right of the person looking at it on a map–Liguria made a real gap, and after tracing its thin, frown shape, the end of Liguria to the east ended in a kind of right angle, which was followed by a descent, and that descent was supposed to be Tuscany, with the province of Grosseto at the bottom, and Calvino's pine forest. But he had not yet found Liguria's right angle. *Was this a trick of the cartographers? Probably*, he told himself.

On a map at the station, he had discovered that the Magra River could, in its own way, identify something of a frontier, an acceptable proposal, and in fact, when he arrived there, he realized almost immediately that that accumulation of fresh water was only flowing to put an end to something.

He also suspected that he was in another place when he was suddenly greeted by dark and very different pine forests, alternating with clearings, and certain small, rather agitated rivers, like the Magra, which were also so different from the other Ligurian streams, on whose shores the sand and gravel banks invented unusual landscapes.

Then he would look around, bewildered and tired, and try to picture something he had already seen, already crossed. And day after day, he sensed a strange modernity in all this. Could time always be blamed? Were these the signs, the climate change that everyone talked about?

One day, skirting the line of a crumbling concrete edge, he reached a small station that must have been far more important in its time, for it was full of now unserviceable tracks and even possessed an old first-class hall. He went to the restroom, as he did first thing when he arrived at stations, to wash himself and quench his thirst, disinfect his scratches. But he was unable to; he needed to pay to use it and he didn't have any money, or rather he had some savings from when he painted the railings in Monterosso, but he didn't want to waste a euro on the restroom. That's all. Come on, one euro to take a piss in a toilet and refresh his neck at the sink?

Surprised, he discussed this with an attendant, asking since when is it fair to charge for public restrooms. Was this another sign of the end of an era and a region?

"How do we deal with this," he said. He looked around, noticing other injustices; for example, that filthy arm rest dividing the bench so as to prevent a passenger from lying down. It was the traveler's sacred right to lie down on the benches.

The attendant listened and laughed. "Old man, the benches are for passengers and you are not a passenger...."

"Oh, I'm not, and what would I be?"

"I don't know what you are, a vagabond, I guess."

Bitter, he did not reply. Sure, he was a vagabond his whole life, and he felt no shame; as for the arrogance of the attendants, he was used to it. In the end, it was only being called an old man that had upset him. Who knows how long he had been one, but this was the first time someone had said it to his face.... *Are you old?* Yet he did not feel old at all...was he therefore an old man? Since discovering that Calvino had died—years spent wandering had passed—something had happened: he had found evidence of the end of Liguria and the impression of his own end, his private end. Yet, how strange, apart from anything else, he did not remember ever being called old man. Old man. He went and looked at himself in a glass window in the first-class waiting room. Yes, time had passed. That's all. A wave, many waves. The attendant had a point. He wished he could have told him, told the whole world about it, admitted it, and confessed to the tracks, "You probably are old." He never died like Calvino, so getting old had been easy. That's all. But in that moment, his words felt old, too.

He had always cut his own hair and shaved himself as best he could with a pair of scissors he found in the garbage a century ago, diligently disinfected in seawater and sharpened occasionally on the tracks. But as time passed, just as he forgot things, one could say he also wound up forgetting the need to look at himself in the mirror. If one could say so.

Now he knew well that Liguria could go on forever, but he was in Tuscany. And at that moment, he felt death so nearby, as if he had felt it every day. He remembered his thoughts on certain nights spent watching the stars with a blade of grass between his teeth, the narrows of the valleys, in the sky, the narrows of the Milky Way. He had grown old dreaming of a woman.

He sat on the divided bench as the attendant continued speaking; there were plenty of people around. He did not want to hear anyone, so he held his head still with his hands. Slowly, the faces and words of familiar people came back to mind, distant fragments.

"It's not like you only met someone who drew islands," the railroad man said. "One time you talked to a guy who took pictures of vegetable gardens and you asked him why. 'Because we had vegetable gardens and they were stolen,' he had said. One day his parents died and because his grandfather was not doing well, they put him in an orphanage. At fifteen he left, at sixteen they took him back and sent him to the frontlines, and when he returned to the village, the children or grandchildren of the people who stole the vegetable gardens were still cunning and each day, he disliked that place more and more; it was a place for tricksters. 'I didn't sell that hole of a house,' he had said to me. He would spend a few days in the countryside–he no longer had gardens of his own–and work to buy what he needed to take photos. The photos remained in his house and one day, the rats would eat everything or there would be a fire and even then, something would survive, something always remained. He was right, even one of my things, some island will remain." He said this to make the people around him laugh, and indeed they laughed, and then he remembered that he did not like being laughed at. In Liguria, or at the bottom of Liguria, one didn't laugh much, one laughed in short bursts.

"During the war, good people, when I climbed through tunnels, the rather grim ones at whose end you can't see a glimmer of light, I would run into the Italian partisans. Not in the tunnels, they usually stood well above, between the cliffs. They would watch the sea and the terraces and the trains; that's all there was, the sea and terraces of olive trees, the tracks...if in the summer, German was spoken more often than Italian, it meant something."

"Let's hear it, what does it mean?" asked one of the waiting passengers.

"That life can change, and as it changes, it passes...Chicù doesn't use the wood and the wood rots...it's a shame, good olivewood...I always tell him that too...sometimes he uses some in September to cook the preserves in the pot...you know, my good people, you fucking railroad worker, you can distinguish the future and the past like the journey between the two stations of time…it's the length of Liguria, the railroads and the restrooms, and the other region. Maybe one of these days, I will find the ocellated lizard and find that it was waiting for me to free itself of its blue skin."

A lady had listened to the discussion and monologue, and, with an untimely delay, agreed with the railroad worker. He was not hurt by this—he was used to it—and shrugged his shoulders, continuing to talk to himself. He cared about the end of Liguria, not the restrooms. No. But she could not have known these things and said, "What if no one paid?"

Tiredly, he answered her.

"Ma'am, wasn't Liguria, for example, the place where the women getting off the train saw me lying on the benches and under the pepper trees?"

The lady walked away, touching her temple with her finger.

That young man, thin and poorly dressed, with eyes of azurite that emerged from some little church deep in the land. The tan of long summers. The women, at that time, would leave a coin on the bench; sometimes they would gather up the courage and slow down so as not to be seen by other passengers, and return to lay a bill on the bench. Generous ladies. Liguria also used to be this, a slightly easier life, less severe. Through the underpass, he would go down for a dip in the sea, and the elderly ladies would greet him. "The young man from the station...."

Because he didn't want to spend money on the restroom and the railroad worker put his foot down, the old man went to urinate in the first bit of darkness in the tunnel. He passed only that track and could glimpse the milky semicircle at the end, and after all, for some time now, most tunnels were short—just a few dozen meters to go through—before the train arrived (he had learned to lay his ear on the track to calculate the distance and he was never wrong), but that day, it had seemed impossible to him to get away with it; he had just discovered he was old, an old man who no longer moved like he once did, and even now as he urinated, he felt a bit more wobbly in the legs.

THE BALL

O ne day, not far from the station where he had been called an old man, at one of those typical Tuscan stations, with its short tunnels and lack of hills behind it and the paid restrooms, as he stood in the middle of the square in front of the building thinking about the regions of Italy, a leather ball stopped between his feet. He tried to return it; missing the kick, the kids held back laughter. He went to sit on the bench under the pine tree and enjoyed watching them.

After a while, a couple of tourists appeared, a woman and a man, possibly from northern Europe because of their fair skin and blond hair. They spoke a little Italian. They were furious.

He asked them, "Because of the paid restrooms?"

"What are you talking about," they tried to explain in broken Italian. They were furious about the strike.

He did not admit it, but strikes did not bother him. In the end, they had only one disadvantage: in the time frame when few trains ran, regular schedules were not respected, and someone like him, informed about every probable delay, ran the danger of being surprised by a freight inside a tunnel, and inhaling grains of filth. He didn't even try to explain this. One of the advantages, however, was that during strikes, many more maintenance crews met on the tracks. He didn't get along with some of the foremen—they wouldn't let him pass—and so all he had to do was resign himself, go up the embankments, set out in search of a cherry tree to pick from, a pond in which to throw the fishing line he always carried with him, until the workers left the site in the evening, at which point he could pass through and see if they had left anything behind. Fortunately, there were also friendly ones among the crews, people who did not give him a hard time; in fact, they shared breakfast with him and allowed him to render a slice of lard over the fire and warm himself.

The northern tourist wore a nice camera around his neck and had laid a pair of binoculars beside him. They took turns adjusting it, pointing it at a horizon scattered with pine trees. The old man explained to them that many years before, he had owned a pair of binoculars himself, a very beautiful blue pair. But the man and woman did not understand. As he spoke, he felt a growing desire to look at the world through binoculars, as he once did. He said that his were a good brand of binoculars which had been given to him by a friend, an island sketcher.

The tourist tried to translate something to her companion and in the meantime, had unwrapped some pieces of focaccia. He accepted, thanking her, and before sharing lunch, he went to wash his hands at the drinking fountain.

They asked him where he was going, and he pointed in the direction of the railroad. The tourist asked, "Florence, Rome?" The old man shrugged his shoulders, feeling a bit ashamed, because in reality, he did not know how to respond. He could have said he was going to Grosseto to visit a friend, but how could he explain such a thing. However, having to say something, he answered, full-mouthed, "Naples-Salerno," for he had heard it many times on the loudspeakers in stations.

After the focaccia (he put it down on the paper suddenly and jerked around to return the ball that had rolled toward the bench to the children, managing to lift it up and kick it with his right foot this time), he went to wash his hands and mouth, hiding his excitement as he walked.

"*Bravo*," said the tourist as he walked back, and her companion added something. He thought he had more or less grasped the meaning, and that the tourist had asked him if he would like to play in a soccer field again.

"We didn't have a field," he said in Italian, "the ball rolled away two out of three times...." Then he admitted, "I would give my life to play with Gino again."

The tourists resumed pointing their binoculars, and when the woman finally put them down, he gathered up his courage, wiped his hands on his shirt, and asked if he could look at something.

He did not look for the sea hiding among the pines, but instead adjusted the binoculars to his old man vision and looked at the mountains. They were white and hollowed out in that scientific way that had intrigued him recently.

The tourist noticed his amazement and said, "*Il blanco de Carraia, señore.*" The old man nodded. He remembered a certain night well, when he was skirting the railroad, at the edge of which there was a large quantity of white slabs piled up. It had started raining and he had sought shelter, not paying too much attention to the strangeness of the place, but attributing that whiteness to the trick of the rain, the lightning, in the night. Even now, the sight of the white mountains seemed to him more a trick of the binoculars and his eyes than the image of a deposit. But perhaps, he told himself as he pointed the binoculars in other directions, couldn't that also be an idea of Tuscany he accepted long ago, without knowing it?

The tourist returned from the drinking fountain with washed plastic cups and poured him hot tea. The old man put down his binoculars, blew on the cup, and after quite a while took a sip and, lost in his thoughts, said nothing more (what was he thinking about?). He was very calm, but when he finished the tea, which he consumed to the last drop, he stood up, as if taken over by a sudden anxiety, thanked them with a half bow, gathered his things, and went in the opposite direction to the one he had pointed to them.

La Spezia

For the first time in his life, he was walking along the same track, but keeping the edge of the sea to his left. Behind him, the loudspeaker at the station was announcing other inconveniences, and he had stopped for a moment to listen. It was news that did not concern him.

His step unsteady because of the discomfort of the slightly sloping gravel, he continued nonetheless with such tried-and-true movements that when he lost his balance, he was able to make up for it in time with a jerk and balance his trunk. The novelty was all in that inevitable sunset, the blue void to the left, and the collapse of the cliffs to the right; he would manage, as he always did.

As for the rest, the gravel maintained the same dusty stony ground as far as the eye could see, smelling of iron, and the slightest skid reminded him of old scrapes.

Arriving near the La Spezia station again, something strange happened and he paid attention to it. An unknown desire, a desire so strong to hurry, seized him, that he went down the underpass, looked at the departure board, and without a second thought, got on the high-speed train to Ventimiglia.

As the train started up, he began to shift in his seat and look out through the glass at the fig trees welded to the walls and to fistfuls of stony earth, and a small cemetery that was followed by vegetable gardens and palm trees, with their pure trunks without branches, as he had seen hundreds of lately.

On the side facing the sea, however, it was a swift passage of furrows of greenery, wedges of vegetable gardens, and uncultivated land blooming with succulents and palm trees. Eventually, the tunnel would surprise him, and while waiting for the light to return the liquid, blue-wrinkled prairie, he had plenty of time to catch himself in the glass window and besides his reflected image, see all the darkness of the tunnel for the first time at the train's speed…what had they been able to sense from inside a carriage, the eyes of the passengers who had caught a glimpse of him for an instant in the light of a floodlight? Nothingness, the same nothingness, in the different seasons of life. They had never been able to recognize him. Had he lived in nothingness in there? Beyond the filter of the glass, tunnel after tunnel, over the years, alone, he had been only a slightly different type of nothingness: the nothingness of a child, an adolescent, the nothingness of an adult and old man, and now an old nothingness on this side of the trench, in the comfortable custody of the carriage, like the last Matryoshka doll.

The roofs of the cities, all gray, and the buildings with their pediments and squiggles, the overpasses, the highways hanging from the cliffs. The sonorous surprise of a squealing brake that had woken him suddenly at night so many times now left on his face the amused and somewhat silly grimace of a passenger. A new, internal noise, his iron heart throbbing steadily and interminably, while out there he had frightened the night away for a single minute.

He imagined the sea rising and everything being overtaken, the cars and vans. He was absorbed by the train's rattling and in the end, sleep overcame him. He sat down on the floor, in the space in front of the carriage, and stayed there, curled up, his knees bent and feet propped up to make room when at one station, a passenger got on the train and stepped over him with his suitcase, apologizing. Once he was in the carriage and had arranged his luggage, the passenger came out to tell him there was an empty seat inside. He shook his head and thanked him; no, he was fine where he was.

He closed his eyes again and felt like sitting down, but the train was crowded and someone was constantly passing through, so he remained standing, his forehead and arms resting against the glass. The journey rocked him into an iron, ancient slumber, until a different screech shook him.

He had never urinated in such pitiful conditions, jolting from one side of the rails to the other, and he felt like laughing. Nothing could be seen through the glass of the bathroom, so he slipped some toilet paper into his backpack, which he had brought with him, and looked at his eyes in the mirror. They had once been the color of the azurite in church frescoes—what did he know about churches, they were not on his path. Sometimes, however, in the summer, looking for a park where he could lie in the shade, he would see a church and go there to sit in the cool air. The people praying intrigued him; after all, didn't they look a little like him? Didn't one pray on one's knees like one went along the tracks? His eyes had slowly lost every glint of blue; they were slits of a phlegm gray, red-veined and crusted. *You're old*, he told himself, *and you're teetering on a train, you're thirsty, and you don't even know if train water is drinkable....*

He heard a knock. "I'm coming out," he said. It was the conductor. He wanted to see his ticket.

He laughed, a ticket? He didn't have one, but he wasn't laughing at that; it was just that the idea of a ticket amused him.

"Do you perhaps have a card?"

The old man laughed again.

"No, not even that, sorry, what kind of card...."

"Where are you going?"

"To Sanremo, to Bresca Square," he said, to be precise.

"And you think that's funny?"

"Sometimes I laugh at nothing, you know...and now I feel like laughing, but I'm laughing at myself, let me be clear."

He thought about those circumstances and that very strange day, in front of a train toilet, without a ticket. When he had begun his service along the railroad, he never imagined that one day he would have turned around and never seen the end of it. The fact was that he was living inside a fable written by Italo Calvino, he said, and the fable's ending was that Calvino was dead and Liguria ended; he might as well go back to Sanremo. "Don't you think so, conductor?" That is why he felt like laughing. Because the tracks never stopped laughing. Since the conductor said nothing and was all too serious, he tried to fix the situation. "It doesn't matter, at the next station I'll take my disturbance elsewhere, if you'll allow me to...."

He looked outside, to hide the return of that irritating giggle, and see where they were. "We're almost in Pieve Ligure, we've done a good part of the route."

"How can you see where we are? I can't even do that, and I pass through here every day...."

"The colors, the plaintive blues of the evening; the poems speak for themselves, I've read so many of them. And then the rocks are different in Pieve, the rocks in Pieve are islands, different little islands; I know them well, believe me, all those islands there. When I used to pass through here, you were still playing with toy trains...."

"I will let you get to Genoa."

"You're generous. I mean it."

"And in Genoa, will you catch a train without a ticket? Don't you have a pension?"

The old man surveyed the passage of the sea, between the villas and the greenery of the pines. He turned around to speak to him. "No, I don't think I'll be catching any more trains...a pension, however, would be nice...."

"Who is waiting for you in Sanremo?"

The old man shifted his gaze to the doorframe of the restroom, and thought about who might still be in Sanremo. But he thought about this often without trying.

"Look, this train stops in Albenga. Go sit down, and when we're there, it'll only be a little longer."

He tilted his head and wished he had said something to this young man, nonsense, for example, "I would have liked a son like that, you know, a conductor on the trains in Liguria. I could have met him now and then at some station, eat a focaccia, briefly say hello, before being apart again." Then, he was always so used to talking to himself that he said it aloud. Even crying, or feeling that railroad sadness, he was so used to that he didn't even notice his tears; he had never been ashamed of experiencing these kinds of things, but now he was a bit. He thought, *What could it depend on, what could cause a similar shame?* He found nothing, no explanation. Did the fact that he was on a train play into it? *Probably, it had to,* he tried to tell himself. Blame it on the circumstances, the train effect that made him cry and laugh like a fool. In the end, he only managed to stop laughing.

"Don't cry," the conductor told him.

"It's just that one gets on the train and lets one's guard down," he said and went back to laughing.

"Go sit down, and keep watch at the window."

The old man went and sat down and looked out through the window. He thought of the islands, which were stars, not the kind that materialized, but the islands that the evening had hidden and the stars that the day had hidden. Of the islands on paper, the ones in library books. One day, in Sestri Levante, he had opened a whole atlas of them. Remote islands. The title was *Atlas of Remote Islands*. The preface, however, was titled *Paradise is an Island. So is Hell.* It was a genre of books that had always tempted him. Stealing it meant getting away with it, but aside from the fruits and vegetables from the gardens and the sun in the winter, and a backpack taken from a shack, long ago, he had never stolen almost anything. Not even the life of beasts. However, he cultivated no good feelings for the little beasts; rather, they stung him, massacred him, left his body an open wound, especially certain species of red spiders on the railroad. He could be in a crevice in a cliff to cool off, or shelter himself from the rain for a day, and see mosses, lichens, and green beetles crawl over his hands and pillbugs huddled together, and the only gesture he was capable of was dividing them if they were killing each other, moving the wounded to safety. The miniscule life in general did not concern him; he already felt himself, his being and his epic, to be something immensely microscopic in relation to the firmament torn apart by the passing iron assault.

Remote islands had different names, double names, it was the language that defined them. For example, the Norwegians called the Island of Solitude *Ensomheden*, while for the Russians it was *Ostrov Uedinenija*, or Island of Retreat. It was located in the Arctic Ocean. It was 20 square kilometers in size and uninhabited. It was discovered in 1778 by E.H. Johannesen.

Islands reached with last efforts. As with Tristan da Cunha, revolutions proclaimed on ships, utopias realized on islands. Islands were the perfect exile.

He had not gotten up again, his elbow resting on the edge of the window held his head.

From time to time, he recognized in the usual marine view all that black emptiness. The end of the tunnel made everything possible again. Like it used to be. It was the nocturnal festival of stations he had already seen. Rapallo. Chiavari. Brignole and Principe, with their pillars, floodlights, rows of electric tubes, and very tall ships in the harbor.

He would have liked to get off at Arenzano; there was a park near the little station in which he had slept for months, sharing the silence with a peacock. But the train did not stop (he would not have gotten off anyway, it was only a desire), as it was a regional high-speed train, the evening one. Torre del Mare and Bergeggi could not be seen from the train—the tunnel passed underneath—and when the train stopped at Spotorno, he went to say goodbye to the conductor and Sbarbaro's verses to his father came to mind.

ALBENGA, AGAIN

The train ended its route on the third platform of the Albenga station. The old man got off and looked for the conductor to thank him. He was at the back of the train, advancing among the few passengers, under the light of the streetlights.

He got off halfway through the train.

"Albenga, ma'am, he who has nothing to do here should not come here," he said to a woman smelling strongly of perfume. The woman lengthened her stride, launching her powerful calves. The old man watched her from behind and nodded, with a certain concern he could not explain.

He waited for the conductor. "I wanted to thank you."

"What are you doing now? Can I offer you something in the cafeteria?"

He dipped his focaccia in his latte and looked around, occasionally smiling, as did his benefactor. Railroad workers did not give alms, they either passed by without looking at you or became your friend.

"I'm leaving in a bit, on the 11:45 p.m. local train. I'll get off at Brignole and wait to change trains," he listed, as if talking to a colleague.

The old man nodded and when they said goodbye outside, he stayed a while on the platform. Then for the second time that day, he went down into the underpass, looked for the last track toward the mountains, which was always the first, and walked west.

He was already tired and his legs ached, but his discomfort did not deprive him of strength; on the contrary, it was as if his legs, left without dreams, were looking for more.

In Punta Murena, having climbed over a barren hill to avoid re-entering the tunnel, he scolded himself for continuing like this. What sense did it make at this point...if the tracks, he knew well, did not end. He might as well abandon them.

The Via Aurelia stretched below him, with a row of streetlights, traffic, comfortable sidewalks, and a guardrail. A temptation, to never again stumble through the graveled, resonant night, to wake the dogs, to have a light from a room or flashlight turned on in his face and be asked where he was going. As if one knew where one was going.

The miracle was Gallinara, the island off the coast of Alassio, faintly lit by a lighthouse. Other lights must have been from boats in calm waters.

Having climbed up again through a landslide, amid shards and garbage of all kinds, clinging to the weeds, he reached a terrace and decided to stop.

From below rose a music that reminded him of his youth spent on the Riviera.

The songs of frogs' orgasms wandered through the air, and he sighed, letting experience dictate his associations: where there are reeds, there is water and where there is water in the summer, there are frogs. After a while, there were no longer many frogs, but a single giant frog.

A bat passed by, just above the reeds, and as it flew further, dodged something, perhaps a cliff or a tree.

"Instead, you return," he said out loud, almost as if trying to convince himself. Before covering himself, he stood up, went to pee, and when he came back to lie down, he fell asleep almost immediately, like children do when they sigh as if talking to themselves.

For several nights, in that reedbed, he dreamed of his young self on the road. He has not left again, and there is no reason to, unless he does not wish to delay his arrival in Sanremo. But why? In any case, in the evening, that reedbed at the end of Alassio, a few terraces above the railroad, welcomed him with its soft, dry carpet of reeds and rags.

Of the places he visited on the trip, he would not know what to say. His dream's structure neglects all geography; he simply moves from city to city, gets off a train, and at the station, they wait for him and take him to play in a soccer field, with the audience in the stands. Therefore in the dream, he is fit, he is young, well-trained, and the scores of the games do not matter, but in the end, he is so tired that someone sleeps next to him because he collapses from exhaustion, and where he throws himself to sleep, he hears the rustle of the reeds fueled by a swish of water every time. He would like to stay awake and not miss anything. These noises represent something magical, an awareness of his physical strength, his health; they are the very soundtrack of his dream, and there is a party down there, at the edge of his dream. *You're fine*, he says to himself, and to prove it, he takes a deep breath and is fine. Oxygen floods his mind.

The leaves of the fleshy-stemmed plants smelled of the creek all the way into his dream. One night, while dreaming the same dream, he distinguished other smells, more specifically, that of the reeds' leaves— not the reeds, but the leaves— which have an earthier smell than the reeds' hard stem, which smells like plastic, and he realized he thought about smelling the sourness of reed leaves as a lively man and an old man. He yawned, his lips half-closed, and a sense of well-being from the dream invaded him, and he stayed for a long time listening to the passage of a train, which died inside the hill of Punta Murena.

It was still nighttime and the sound of frogs defiled the bright silence of summer and everything, even the waves, under the Via Aurelia, so equal to and different from each other, belonged perfectly to that silence.

He stood there and knowing only that he would leave during the day, he reached for his bag with his hand and then for his water bottle. He swallowed a long gulp. His jacket was dry, as every night the reeds had protected him from the dew. When he felt it was time, he straightened up and took it off. He also freed himself of one of his shirts because it was already hot. He folded and stuffed everything into his backpack with the rest of his belongings, slung it over his shoulder, and resumed the descent to the railroad that was not yet clear.

The first night in the reed bed, he had woken up, as he did now, to resume his walk, and realized that at the end of the terrace, there was no stream; the frogs' home was all the water collected in pots, which was used for irrigation. It came down from the mountains in black plastic pipes, and the excess was lost in rivulets that facilitated the growth of reeds. But tonight, he had forgotten all about this and as the sound of water entered his dream, he imagined a small stream again.

He looked at the reed bed and concrete pots. Dawn was arriving from the east, and for the first time, he walked with his back to it.

It was impossible to find the right words to describe how beautiful

Alassio was. He had read about one writer, an exile or deserter who had lived in Portugal for a long time, who had called Lisbon sparkling. That's it, Alassio was sparkling, and he had always wanted to return to it. To look for Chicù's shack, to hear if beyond the window the moon still snored. To ask about the sketcher of islands. Who knows, he was around twenty years older than him and he was an old man.

He stopped and let his arms hang down at his sides in front of the rocks of the Coscia Tower where the island man had given him swimming lessons…if he ever saw him again, he would tell him everything, and he would answer his questions, starting by admitting that he had not found the end of the tracks, because the tracks are infinite; they cross mountains and fertile valleys, as that Duilio Cossu claimed, forests of stars and bricks, they skirt the sea foam of beaches of other sparkling regions. And for all these reasons, the end of the tracks could no longer rush or even frighten him. He would have told him that.

Should he return to Sanremo? Maybe, although he did not need to think about it now; returning there was only a small matter. And the sketcher of islands would have agreed.

He did not feel like cooling off in the sea; there was time. To find another mule path, he remembered that one had to continue a stretch along the tracks. At one point, there was a level crossing, and beyond the Via Aurelia, the mule path that led to Solva.

He did not remember it being so steep; every now and then, he had to stop to take a breath and get his bearings. In fact, it seemed to him that he no longer recognized anything; the vegetable gardens should have started at this point, as well as the dozen dusty olive trees around Chicú's shack.

He asked a couple of men, not too young, who had come out of a rolling shutter in shorts and sneakers, about to start their jog. The two listened and gave a slight smile, amazed. A shack, with tomatoes? Chicú and a sketcher of islands?

He grew impatient and confirmed everything; it was useless for them to repeat everything he said. The island man had a villa, the concrete joints between two rows of stones.

And where was the mansion, did he know? The two men asked together.

No, he said, he had never seen the villa in real life, only in a drawing, and he had not wanted to sleep there because of a personal matter, which had nothing to do with this conversation, but he did not mind talking about it: he did not want to stray from the railroad, that's all.

In short, he had slept in Chicú's shack.

The two men listened, hands on their hips, about to start their jog.

The island man was named Carlo and was a good artist. And he must have been fine, he said, trying to hold them back a moment longer. He had given him a pair of lightly used sandals that had broken after two months and he tied them with string, but they kept breaking, so he threw them away. They had not broken because they were of poor quality—he makes sure to clarify—he was the one who by dint of walking on the gravel of the railroads, deformed his shoes.

One of the two men said maybe they could help him. Alassio was unrecognizable, but a villa with a pine forest and stone walls.... Then he explained again that he didn't want to go to the villa; he was interested in Chicú's shack and to know if Carlo had ended up like the shack, but he had, for sure.

At the end of a discussion among them, the athletes said that they didn't know anything about a shack, but that they understood whose villa it was. It was Carlo Levi's villa and he had been dead for at least forty years. He had been a painter and a writer, and before or during the war, he had been in exile, one of them said.

"He had been in exile before the war," the other pointed out.

"When did you meet him?"

"Not immediately after the war," he said, "I met him when I was already a man."

The two men liked the division of time, before and immediately after the war.

The old man saw them laughing and it seemed to him a bit like they were making fun of him. However, they immediately made themselves very useful, each took out their cell phones, and looked for a photograph of Carlo Levi. The old man put on his glasses, got closer to one of the cell phones, brought his fingers to his lips, and took a small step back.

The sketcher of the islands was thus Carlo Levi.

It must have been about noon when he climbed the marble stairs of the library.

He asked, with a slightly urgent tone, if he could please see Carlo Levi's books and photographs. He expected to be made to sign a paper, as was the case with library requests, but the lady tilted her head to one side and asked him, "I'm sorry, what photographs?" She asks her colleague, "Do we have a collection of photographs of Carlo Levi?"

In the meantime, another librarian had arrived and this man said that the Carlo Levi picture gallery was in the Palazzo Morteo and had a good number of canvases, photographs, and drawings.

"That's what we told him," said one of the female librarians.

"Okay, and what kind of drawings?"

The three librarians looked at each other and the male one said, "Well, of many things: animals, nature, lots of plants, carob trees...."

"And islands, did he draw any?"

"I don't think so, maybe, but he drew so many things, and there are his letters and notes, and even a reproduction of a portrait he had done of Calvino...."

"Calvino Calvino? The writer? You mean they were friends?"

The women responded. "Of course they were, Calvino used to visit him in Alassio, in Levi's villa...."

The old man lowered his eyelids and saw him smoking again, on the rocks at the Coscia Tower.

The male librarian was talking to himself, as the old man was hardly paying attention, and the questions were echoed by the female librarians as well: they wanted to know whether he was sure that his friend the sketcher of islands was Carlo Levi, because if he was, that was important. And he said yes, of course he was sure. It was him, gosh.

He jotted down the address of the villa on a piece of paper, despite the fact that the ladies had printed everything out for him, including photos and other things. Before taking the underpass again, he sat on the edge of a low wall, his forearms on his thighs, and took to reading some of the printed things and studying the photos of the house.

After a slight slope, the road to Solva went up the hill between the villas, until on the left a wall covered with vines rose up and on the right the road skirted a fence. In the distance, he could see a gate, a row of pine trees, and a villa. He looked for a photograph of Levi's villa; almost everything matched. Yes, the wall was not stone, or maybe it was but from a distance he could not tell. The shutters were brown like the door, and the building could have been said to be composed of two sections built during different time periods; there were even two roofs side by side.

He stopped and laid his arms on the last stretch of fence; no one could go beyond that. So he turned around and took another ramp. Wisteria grew next to the old fence and the old man hung his backpack on a board, brushing the vegetation. As he rested, he asked a passerby for information, but this man knew nothing. The second person passing by, a man with a puppy, said that Carlo Levi had died in 1975, he was a famous writer, they had sent him into exile, and the old man stopped him; he knew these things, everything was in the papers and even the photos. What he wished was to talk to someone who had known him. "But I know it won't be easy," he said.

From that moment, as the man with the little dog responded to his request, explaining that there was in fact a possibility, the old man felt a feeling of hope grow. The man had taken a few steps aside and was calling on his cell phone.

"They'll answer me," he said.

"I'm sorry, who will answer you?"

"A lady's son," said the man who had shut off his cell phone and returned to the old man. The little dog did not feel like standing there on the sidewalk, listening to them talk, and pulled him. The man let go of the leash a little and before tugging it back toward him, he smiled.

"Did you know Carlo Levi?" the man asked.

The old man said you bet, he had even given him binoculars and drawings, sandals, all lost, he hastened to point out. "You bet I knew him."

The woman had stayed in her garden. Beyond the railing, the old man hung his backpack on the gate. The house was not far; it was a beautiful house and the woman must have been beautiful too. At that point, the gentleman with the puppy said goodbye to everyone, and the old man thanked him. On the front steps, a young man appeared, raised his hand as well, and said in dialect, "Grandma, I'm in the garage, call me if you need me, or come in that way."

The sea, visible from almost everywhere in Alassio, remained behind the hill from that point, and the woman, if she did not look seriously at the old man, hinted a resigned smile as of someone who has spent their life searching for the sea. Because the man with the puppy had informed her about the old man's request, the woman said she had been friends with a little girl who lived in the house of letters. She always called it that, the house of letters, but she could not remember the origin of that name. Maybe, she said, it was the little house where Mr. Levi's mail arrived? Certainly her friend's father's expertise was that of a sharecropper, tending the grounds of Villa Levi and doing other small jobs or deliveries for Carlo Levi.

The old man did not interrupt her until the woman recounted that she often went to the villa's park with her friends, but not into the villa, and that walking among the plants, they would see Mr. Levi leaving with determination with his easel and painting supplies.

"And did you talk to him?"

"No, almost never, we were little girls, but Mr. Levi smiled at us. He always had a cigar in his mouth and that half-sad smile, but when his friends came to visit him he laughed very much and seemed like a different person, less sad, in fact, not at all."

"He also made a portrait of Calvino, you probably saw him too. In fact, that's what I wanted to know."

The woman said, "I've read Calvino's books, at least one for sure, but I don't remember the title...he certainly visited Mr. Levi, but I, at the time, did not know who was who among his guests...."

"And you say they laughed, Calvino and Carlo Levi? You listened to them, and do you know what they were laughing about?"

"They did. I can't say what they were talking about, we were in the back playing. They were looking at the sea, which was visible from where they were, as well as the island of Alassio—that's what we call it."

"I know."

"No, I can't say what they were laughing about...."

"If they were looking at the island, they would also have seen the railroad."

"No, you can't see the railroad...they also had a telescope which they pointed around."

"Then they also saw Corsica."

"Oh, certainly at sunset, because it's at sunset that it comes out."

He asked her when she was born and did the math.

"I'm doing the math," he told her.

"What math?"

"I think and the math comes by itself."

"What are you thinking about?" asked the slightly irritated woman.

"I'm thinking about how old I could have been when you heard the sketcher of islands and Calvino laughing."

"What sketcher...is it that important to know whether they were laughing?"

"It is fundamental, ma'am. If they were looking at the sea with the telescope and toward the hill where the trains enter, and they were laughing, then yes, it is very important."

Alassio Station

In front an escarpment, not far from the streets perpendicular to the sea, he lowered a branch and touched some fruits. They were unripe and already poisoned by the pollution coming from the train and cars. The fig tree peeped out, shading the asphalt, and the air smelled salty.

The old man walked until he found himself—after the Via Aurelia—at the sea. Since there was not a single public beach, he was forced to enter an establishment, through the colorful gate, and leave his duffle bag a few steps from the shore. He had not even taken off his shoes before the lifeguard scolded him, telling him to move his duffle bag and go to the public beach.

The old man scratched his ear and complained that he couldn't find any. "Then move your ass and take your bag," said the lifeguard.

The old man felt like laughing, remembering the endless stubs in the poems, and repeated, "Move your ass and go away." But he did not obey. In fact, he took off his shirt.

What did this tanned, muscular lifeguard know about the survival techniques of an old railroad pilgrim? He searched his duffle bag for his shorts and went to the changing room, his skinny legs much whiter than his chest, his injured feet burning on the sand.

The lifeguard meanwhile had climbed down from the watchtower and waited for him to return on the shore.

"What did I tell you?"

"To move my ass."

He walked past him with his head down and took a few steps into the water. He winked and smiled.

"Watch my backpack, it's all I own, and just in case, stop the wave for me...."

Before diving under, he threw lots of water over his bony shoulders. The water was chilly, and the requiem of the wave caressed his thighs, giving him a shiver. He looked around and saw that he was surrounded by children. Balls, however, did not bounce. A couple of mothers watched him a bit worriedly, from a proper distance. He wanted to reassure them and smiled. He continued, as if to gather courage, washing his shoulders and neck, his legs and stomach, laboriously lifting one foot and wiping it between his fingers—even the lifeguard was keeping an eye on him—and finally, he plunged in.

He recalled in waves, while plunging in and out of the water, the days when the waters of the Bagni Paradiso formed a natural pool and his mother would get a changing room for them. He waved his arms at his sides, as if he had to move something to proceed underwater. But what? The days of his life that jumbled together? But were there that many? They certainly must have been light, otherwise he would not have been able to move them from where they were. Although each season was supposed to have a distinct weight, they contained too many blockages of sunsets laid on the horizon, and some seasons even had a railroad tied to their foundation, and if one were not careful swimming underwater, one might swim headfirst into something, which is why he preferred to swim with his eyes open.

A beautiful lady, with no children around her, prepared herself for a kind of elegant and calm dive. As she emerged, disguisedly, she barely pressed her dripping breasts for a moment.

The old man noticed this and smiled at her. She did not return it. Nor did she understand when he said to her, "Ma'am, how is it that all of a sudden underwater one feels such melancholy...." And the old man did not insist. He splashed the water, pondering.

Calvino had hinted at the railroad fable, so they laughed? Probably. Why they had laughed, he did not know, but one can laugh as one laughs at an oddity: long ago, the island sketcher had been told by Calvino the story of the pilgrim child, and one day, he had pointed out the coincidence to him and explained that he had met that pilgrim. At the Coscia Tower, he had met someone who was practicing his swimming technique; he was from Sanremo, and all his life, since childhood, walked along the railroad. There, at that point, Calvino might have stopped laughing—not immediately—and touched his forehead, questioning the miracles of literature...and from that day on, a glance exchanged between them would be enough to feel like accomplices and unleash a laughter whose reasons no one else would have understood.

But now, in all that water full of liquid melancholy, he did not feel like laughing, for the whole world had laughed at him and his demons.

When he emerged from his fifth or sixth dive, instead of returning to the shore, he walked a little further out to sea. A few lazy strokes followed, and where he could no longer touch the bottom with his toes, he turned over and floated on his back, his shoulders toward the island, to see the hill of Solva.

The old woman had revealed something terrible to him. A kind of betrayal. Because the fact that Calvino and Carlo Levi had laughed at him was a betrayal. They looked at the hill, the knoll above the tunnel, and laughed....

Had it been in the villa's park, among the pine trees, that Carlo Levi had painted Calvino's portrait? Even that she could not tell him; how could that old woman know? But it must have been so, yes, in the park, and at sunset, they would look for things in the distance and laugh.

Only one person in the world has not laughed at you.

One swam on that expanse of sand wrinkled like an old man's forehead, and underwater, open eyes were nourished with melancholy, coral, and the corpses of small crustaceans.

When he returned, he noticed that the lifeguard's shouts were directed at him. But he wasn't worried; he breathed calmly, as if he were already out of touch with reality. His memories of the Bagni Paradiso dissolved in the strange saltwater of Alassio dripped from his nostrils and eyes. He tasted a sip of the water; not sweet but not salty either, it was barely brackish. How was that possible?

He spat after performing a resounding gargle. The women looked at him. "It disinfects the throat," he said, amused. He hinted a smile at the lifeguard as he walked past him, searched his backpack for a T-shirt to dry his hair, and waited for the air to dry the rest of his body. The lifeguard had climbed back up to the watchtower, and the old man raised his face and spoke to him. "Hey, it seems to me that there is something missing on this beach—is there something missing?"

"What do you think? Last year, the sea swallowed up a row of umbrellas." No longer grumbling, he suddenly seemed more docile.

After putting on his shirt, the old man ran his hand over his cuffs and sleeves and straightened out a few wrinkles. He rarely did this, but today he was leaving Alassio for the second time and it was a special occasion. He adjusted his collar, slung his backpack over his shoulder, and held his shoes and socks in one hand.

Next to the wooden staircase was a faucet and basin. He washed his feet, lengthening his stride so as not to put them back in the sand, and sat down on the step. He removed some of the sand between his toes and, as his ankles dried in the sun, took a long look at the beach and the island. From the watchtower, the lifeguard was busy dealing with some disobedient beachgoers.

He thought of Carlo Levi's exaggerations and reason for attributing a different island to each altitude. He shook off his socks unhurriedly, and the scent of wood from the changing rooms, bar soap, and sunscreen also became the timeless reasons.

He wore old moccasins because his boots, which he carried in his backpack, made him too hot in the summer. They were covered in dust, so he went back to the faucet, turned on a row of them, and rubbed the shoe's leather upper. He washed his hands again with the bar soap, which was about to melt in the saucer. As the soap released its final essence, he smelled it for a long time and lowered his eyelids. "Are you done?" said a lady with a child.

The sidewalk by the Muretto of Alassio was an anthology of tiles dedicated to singers, writers, actors, musicians, and sportsmen. He had read a few of these names in magazines abandoned on the benches, recognized some faces from his city's festival. He knew the faces of some, not even the voice of others. Several were no longer around.

"One chases corals underwater," he told a couple of passersby. The two smiled and kept walking. He would have liked to talk to someone about it, the two who were walking in front of him. Where was he going? Was he really returning to Sanremo? "What did my inventor have in store for me, good people, to make you laugh some more? Do I get to Sanremo, graze the city, and keep going? Do I get on a train, without a ticket, and get off at Port Bou, or while I'm at it, keep going until I reach Lisbon?"

But the idea of Sanremo fascinated him too much. *In my opinion, it is your duty to stop in Sanremo. It is destiny, you go back to the beginning of the fable because that is your destiny. And it's no laughing matter. You are one who obeys. That's all.*

But one time in Tuscany, he was asked to rethink himself.

At the end of the underpass, he walked up the stairs to his platform. His eye fell on the ticket stamping machines and it occurred to him that he, too, had always seemed to be stamping a ticket.

The Alassio station was beautiful, with its concrete benches and small arbors. It was a festival of tracks in every sense: a double headed rail, with insulated rail joints for electrical circuits; continuously welded, elastic rail clips, plated and bolted. He knew these things, as well as the times when the maintenance crews used herbicides; it was around May, sometimes earlier. He knew on which days the leaves would fly on the tracks. He knew in which freight yards he would sleep if the cold froze them, and a few months later, he would touch them to feel them burning and be able to tell himself that he didn't understand anything anymore because it seemed to him that time had flown by, but instead he had only walked from one little station to the next. In the marshalling yards where they broke down the trains, he sometimes found a blanket or a half bottle of brandy hidden by the crane operator. He recognized the previously running locomotives that were one day inexplicably abandoned. He knew the movements of the graffiti gangs: they were usually peaceful, but not all of them. He had not always defended himself; once he had been savagely beaten. But on other occasions, he had had to break a bottle because they would have killed him. He was a loner, and the tracks were there for everyone.

He hopped on the creaking gravel, feeling a strange exhaustion from the start. Yet he had rested, the swim and the sun had invigorated him, the Muretto of Alassio and the sight of the beautiful women by the sea had put him in a good mood. What was it then, the knowledge that he had been the brunt of Carlo Levi and Calvino's joke? This again? No, it was the residue of something else, an exhaustion that encamped in the previous days, of accepting the idea of the infinity of the tracks. Consciousness.

He stopped to look at a pair of stub tracks, tossed in the clearing, that did not count, that were no longer needed. Laughable. Not dead tracks, they were just stubs, because a stub track still retained an image of infinity, and the poetry of infinite stubs.

THE END OF THE TRACKS

Before falling asleep in the usual reedbed to the west, he listened to the night. There were frogs, as there were before he reached Alassio, and the air smelled of the creek and maidenhair ferns. He had walked a lot uphill that day, a day full of surprises, and he became sleepy almost immediately.

At dawn, he looked for Corsica and shrugged his shoulders. If it was not there, he was unlikely to see it at sunset.

A long stretch of the tracks was not far from the sea and in the night, he had heard the waves. The beaches were covered by a row of buildings, and toward the mountains, the railroad distributed yards, fences, canopies, and a small vegetable garden from whose walls the branches of a lemon tree peeked out. Certain railroad plants took root in the concrete and the gravel. They fed on the earth's tremors and their leaves absorbed the rust.

It occurred to him to squeeze a lemon into the water bottle and quench his thirst for the whole day, but it would have been too complicated. He would have had to climb the low wall and latch on to the wired fence. It was daytime, and sooner or later, someone would look out from the balconies of the buildings.

The tunnel appeared around a slight bend, not far from the town of Laigueglia, and by that time, he had already begun to think about how to ascend the hill.

The ups and downs through the narrow, gated passages took him a short distance from the tracks, and one by one, although everything had changed, he recognized the places that, many years before, he had traveled through in the opposite direction.

There was so much talk of Calvino's lopsided Liguria: all crumbly and full of ascending steps, gradations, sequences. But his Liguria, the region dreamed up for him, even the hill he was ascending, ended up drawing only a double straight line, sometimes imperceptibly curving and perfectly boring, with level crossings and undergrounds in which underpasses and substations rested. Somewhere in the library, he had read that in describing his own obsessions, his creator had smeared the hills of Sanremo with objects, buildings, and other steps raised haphazardly.

He had not liked *Invisible Cities*. And he had pitied those who had wasted so much time writing books about those invisible cities. He had only known construction sites of cities, and in watching these cities grow, his life had passed by, to the extent that the buildings and houses, now that he was returning to the childhood of the tracks, appeared to him as precarious and old as he was. Discolored objects, waiting for restoration or total demolition, to make space for other novelties, other narrative objects.

Until something unexpected happened. At the bottom of the Cervo hillside, past the plaza from which the fishermen had dreamed of the corals of the Sanguinaires, and then down through the last crooked, flowery stairways, he, in that epic of porticoed nostalgia, desperately searching for points of reference, did not find them. He found nothing. There was the tunnel, the gravel pavement, the walls with rusty latticework, even the lemons. And there were no more tracks.

He entered the darkness and searched for matches—he always had a couple of boxes of them with him. He lit one after another, not remembering such a long tunnel. He detested tunnels. In fact, he had hardly ever gone through any; he would go through the first few meters and if he found spaces on the side, he would squeeze through them. He would never go through the whole tunnel though, unless it was a very short distance and the arc of light guaranteed enough space or a walkable concrete edge. Without these conditions, he would go up the hill, but by now it didn't matter. The tunnel did not have tracks or trains and the darkness magnified the noises. Much more water flowed than inside an active tunnel and drafts seeped in from everywhere and extinguished his matches. A tunnel unused for years and now in ruins.

He continued even after he had used the last match, bending over now and then to feel the wet gravel and search for the icy iron of the track and crossties with his hand, but there was no need; he would have felt them under his feet. And they weren't there. A tunnel rotted from the rain, the long groove, and the short, crosswise grooves, left by a prehistory of crossties and tracks, a toothless gum.

He returned west at first, to the growing light from the entrance to Cervo, and was greeted by little more than the pallor of a pine sunset. Up there, ahead of him, was Cape Berta and before it, Diano and San Bartolomeo. He went in slow steps, seemingly tired, his heart puffing more than usual and his throat burning.

The most banal effect of a railroad despoiled of its tracks lay all in that one absence, and despite the fact that everything was silent and the air no longer trembled, getting used to the idea of a deserted railroad was not easy. He walked constantly fearing that at any moment, by some infernal and absurd railroad hoax, a crazed train might come up behind or in front of him, creeping over the gravel, as if by inertia, destined to derail within a few feet of his ankles. A journey forced to halt its momentum in the escarpment. He leaned out. The shrubs hid wrappers and bottles, the Via Aurelia passed below or next to the railroad, and the sand and the sea were even further below, beyond the buildings.

He found the Diano Marina station, an orphan of the railroad, boarded up and deserted, the gravel leading to the entrance of a tunnel topped by Cape Berta, the end of which he could barely see. The more he penetrated it, the more he heard the sound of the gravel crunching under his step, the echoes caused by the seepage of water.

When light exploded in the distance, a widening, largely occupied by piles of tracks and guard rails, materialized to his right, and he heard a grunt. A boar?

He tiptoed out and his eyes had not yet adjusted to the light before darkness greeted him again.

The grunts stopped. He was walking on bottle shards and whole bottles were rolling in the grooves. He decided to change his moccasins for some beat-up boots whose soles were coming off. *These are on their last leg*, he always thought, and yet they were better for walking on glass.

He started talking out loud to hear the echoes.

You see the light at the end, you see it? It's not too far, it's just that up there it curves....

He fiddled around with his thoughts, exercising his reddened eyes adjusted to the dark.

It is the last light of the day.

In fact, it was the last timid slip of a burnt silence.

Now you remember what western sunsets are. And you are hungry and thirsty....

Among the things in his backpack, his hand sought the cylindrical shape of the bottle, which he sipped from, leaving some for later. He knew well that under normal circumstances, every fifty steps could be counted by the yellow light of a floodlight. But aside from the dangerous boars, the rest, including that complete darkness, no longer worried him. *You became an old man underground.*

A mutilated railroad had no more secrets. His foot had learned to avoid stumbling in the groove and he paused to listen to the echo of words again, separated from that of his footsteps. His back to the wall, his hands found the muddy coating on the stones. The dripping silence was populated with wingbeats: bats, insects. He tapped the ground with his boots first to make sure there was no glass and then let himself continue along the wall. Near it, the old electricity pipes ran inside the concrete edge. He sat down next to it and with his toes, pressed down on the base of the gravel rising to form the hump.

What if in a little while you come out, what if you give up everything?

He felt like laughing.

Let's say they are there. If you were soon to stumble on the rails, what would he ask you to do? Would you go that way? Admit it, you would definitely disobey him. Wasn't finding the beginning of the rails finding the end of them?

Exhaustion—nothing else, not thinking—was a kind of torture that lasted for almost a century.

Sometimes, at night, in front of the sea foam and his desires, on the fright of the entire sea, he wondered what was there, not beyond the tracks at the end of the railroad, but beyond a rail system directed far beyond Sanremo, to a more distant west, which he had not chosen and in which, at some point, as occurs in Spain, beyond the border of Port Bou the rails are wider or narrower to prevent an invasion.

Of the pictures he looked at in the books and magazines of the publishing house where Calvino had worked, he remembered some of a Jewish-German author (he had never read him, just his name, Walter Benjamin, and some headline about his sad end) who wore round glasses and traveled through Europe. When he was born from Calvino's dreams, Benjamin was in Sanremo and would stay there on several occasions before the war. He was unaware of these things and only knew that Benjamin's journey was interrupted at Port Bou, where the railroad system was interrupted. And since no one ever informed him, he would never have imagined that it was on this man, on Benjamin, that his interest in the ocellated lizard depended. It was Calvino who had told Carlo, the island sketcher, about it and told him that as children, he and Benjamin had searched for it. The story of the blue lizard had fascinated Carlo Levi and then the old man. Having resumed his journey to the east, with his binoculars he sifted through cliffs and stony ground, the greens and pinks of the cisti, and the blinding blue of the sea and sky. He had seen it, but not in person; the ocellated lizard had visited him during feverish nights. He had seen that fierce saurian eye, heard it laughing silently, smelled its putrefying odor....

To be on the other side of the railroad system and see his father, of whom he could remember almost nothing, and his mother, maybe even Gino, and the old man, that old man from Tuscany who on the bench in Bresca Square threatened to puncture the ball if it passed by him again.... "*Forare, sfiorare*[7], what language do you speak," Gino asked him.

"Oh, dumb little Gino, you know you are really ugly," retorted the old man.

"I have arrived, dad, mama. Friends of Bresca Square, I'm here...." "Congratulations idiot," they would have told him. Maybe life on the other side is just the magic of hearing things; there comes a silence of music and voices, and everything that over here one says and thinks about someone on the other side is perceived on the other side, which is why, once on the other side, one apologizes profusely to the dead. Apologies accepted. They too when they were alive thought who knows what strange things of the dead, not very nice things, you know, the things of the lives of the living about the lives of the dead when

---

[7] In Italian, *forare* means to puncture and *sfiorare* means to graze. These specific words are not commonly used in everyday Italian.

they lived.... In Liguria, they say, *parlandone da vivo*[8], so they can do just that. And maybe even on the other side they say things about the lives of the living, but when a recently dead person comes along, will the dead apologize to him?

You don't want to lose contact with your sense of direction, do you? What do you say? He took a sip. He looked for something to support himself on with his hand and hoisted himself up laboriously. He poured some water on his hands, and continued forward.

---

[8] This Ligurian proverb means that one may speak ill of a dead person as long as they talk about them as if they were still alive.

Oneglia and Port Maurizio

The clean, warm air catapulted him onto the chuckle of the sea.

The Galeazza beach crumbled by landslides of walls, and the villas and pines hemmed in to the east a piece of the bay on which gleams and blotches, seemingly the color of the earth, floated all the way to the horizon. And well above must have sat Cape Berta and Alpicella, but he did not know it.

Before the Oneglia town signs, the gravel penetrated another tunnel. The station was hardly lit, the doors were closed with boards and chains, grass grew on the platform, and a number of rails were piled along the freight yard. A mess of other materials reigned everywhere: loose and coiled cables, rusting locomotives. The walls were covered with writing.

He sat on a bench on platform 2 and stared at the naked grooves. Here and there, instead of rails, they had laid black rubber pipes. He looked at them and quenched his thirst.

Port Maurizio appeared at the foot of the hill, embedded with lights, and above the railroad track, a car with sirens often sped by on the Via Aurelia. Besides the gravel, nothing remained of the period during which he had crossed that stretch of tracks. They had not even saved the purple toll booth buildings; they were turned into cottages, painted green and pink, the Ligurian colors, with gardens and canopies, and equipped with a gate instead of a level crossing.

A row of maritime pines peeped out from the Via Aurelia, whose needles, dangerously bent over the gravel, released the nocturnal buzz of cicadas. The noise from the traffic alternated with the swish of the sea.

Beside the railing of the obsolete level crossing near the foot of the hill, he paused to read a billboard bolted high on the wall. A light-colored crust, surmounted by the light of a lamppost: ancient rust dripped from the bolts and square blocks of stone.

He stood below it and slowly repeated aloud, as a child would have read it.

Por-t Mau-ri-zio.

He remembered the station well. Quite a few exotic trees had survived, which must have seemed much larger to him now, or conversely, when he had seen them, they might have just been planted. The tallest plants—the ones with the shiny leaves—partly hid the Parasio cliff, embedded with green lights, and the Cathedral of San Maurizio which gave the impression of a spaceship.

He didn't bother looking for the toilets and went directly to the pile of tracks. In the widening before the tunnel, he urinated.

He took a short walk under the lampposts. The type of crossties that were removed was the one with the bolted hooks. He hated that type of crosstie. Once as a child in the summer, he was walking along the tracks barefoot and his right foot got caught in a hook. He bent down and lifted one up. He had never understood the usefulness of these hooks. He tried to take it off the crosstie, but it was impossible. It was as if it were welded there, even though it was moving side to side and up and down, almost freely.

On the other hand, the only things that remained were those too difficult to remove from a dead station: a fountain and an etched concrete basin, the kind that holds goldfish; the dozen plants that had grown sideways, not upwards, as if by an accumulation of desolations and saps from who knows what parallel life. These roots traveled uncovered, raising the pavement and strangling an extensive collection of gutters and railings.

He decided to spend the night under the canopy, on the only bench that had survived vandalism. He rolled up his ragged shirt like a pillow and kept his jacket on hand to lay over his shoulders if he got cold. He tied the bag to the rope and the rope to his wrist—his ritual of retreat—then tucked the rope underneath himself to hide it. They would have had to yank him to rob him.

In his sleep, he thought he had heard a rooster, but that was impossible; the building was located in the center of the city. He had not suffered from the cold and daylight quickly materialized a familiar landscape full of locales with broken glass windows and messy walls, and piles of tracks and guard rails glittering in the sun.

Volumes of plants filled with roots and shorter, stubby palms sprouted from the stairways, chosen to replace the corpses of the amputated palms, which were usually taller and thinner. The decapitated palms, however, remained and cast a long shadow on the asphalt. Someone waiting for dawn at the station had told him that lately, a small animal had been enjoying devouring the hearts of the palms. A small animal that enjoyed eating palm trees, come on. Then, he had inquired in the library and found out that it was so; there was a small animal with a terrible spile and hungry for tender palm wood.

Railroad plants grew in masses or met a killer.

He knew the insects of the countryside well. The clock of animal noises worked almost better than the clock of light; the summer insects filled every hour of the night and day with different buzzes. Insects and frogs took turns, then the blackbirds and nightingales. Only later was it the seagulls' turn.

The tracks were gone, disappeared even from imagination, and the old man yawned.

There were dust and chains on the doors and shutters of the Port Maurizio station. Everything was boarded up, including the waiting rooms and the old café. In the control room, they had forgotten some greasy and unserviceable small machinery, levers, power sockets, and disconnected wires. He looked in from the outside, face pressed against the glass and palms cupping the sides of his face.

He felt a great desire to go back up the steps and walk down the street of stores that he thought he had already walked down–lately he was confusing everything, beaches, squares, stations–and he wasn't sure he had. It's the syndrome of returning, he told himself. But then the desire left his mind.

Beyond the steps, a couple of smaller, paved streets started from the Via Aurelia, with a palm tree at each storefront. One of the streets made a horseshoe shape, and toward the west, in the afternoon, on the white facade of a theater, with its marble and cornices, the sun would die. The road then descended through a groove between the buildings and reencountered the Via Aurelia, the tracks, and the bank of an ever-dry stream.

Ditching the gravel track to go through the streets of Port Maurizio would have meant taking a longer route and going around the hills, not knowing if somewhere inside the tunnel the tracks would begin again. As he entered the darkness, he realized that he was thinking about death and dead tracks and other such final things. An oddity because he hardly ever wondered about death. Rather, the register his inventor imposed was that of a child's exploration of the world. It was a register used by an innocent person; the wonders and the palm trees, the islands and the moon, and that sunset the child and his mother watched on the terrace of Sanremo.

The salty residue that hovered over the old station had given way to the old, damp smell of a cave. As a young man walking below, he would have looked up at the dripping water and wondered: who knows who lives up there? Maybe the child who sleeps in his crib hugging a ball. But that was not thinking about death.

He emerged at the Prino river and wished to rest a while, although the stretch of the tunnel he had walked was short. His arms on the railing, he looked at the sea foam and then at the valley. On the backboard that closed off the Prino Valley like a gate, Calvino had been a partisan, and maybe it was there that he had imagined Pin's adventures and journeys. He felt like going down the steps and into the water, but could not decide; maybe because he was fine where he was. The sun warmed him and he could see a bit of the mountains and a bit of the sea, and the morning passed without his noticing. When he set out again and looked at the city, he saw that the green shutters in the majestic plaster of Parasio shone, and the shadows of the balconies were oblique clippings. And beyond all this, he was now hungry, and along and under that stretch of gravel there was nothing, not a kiosk nor a vegetable garden.

At the bottom of the next cliff, the long incision that had once been the railroad formed other small pebble beaches. To the east, the extension of the Port Maurizio pier was surmounted by white lighthouses. Before the tunnel, he took the underpass that led to one of the beaches and descended the steps.

At the Height of the Ferrocarril

Using the underpass was an instinctive and rather trivial gesture. What was the point; if one refused to cross the tracks, but then could no longer find them, a contract would be broken....

As a young boy, he used to play a game of stepping from one crosstie to the next. The perfect stride, the back foot remaining one moment in the past and the other, on the outer edge of the next crosstie, resting in the future. The crossties used to be made of wood, equipped with stupid hooks; now they made them with prestressed concrete, a State Railroad engineer had explained to him. The equally stupid markings, acronyms, and codes, engraved on the concrete, on the other hand, remained a mystery. Perhaps they were for apprentices as he had been, and indicated a calculation, a step regulator. For example: for a child, it was an A-B-A-B step, while an adult's stride was longer: the past on the edge of crosstie A, the present flew over B, and the foot stopped on the edge of C.

The length of the old man's stride, on the other hand, became uncertain, and the unexpected could occur: from A, his foot would stop on crosstie B, or it would continue on and in its momentum, go on to skim the edge of C. But from San Bartolomeo onward, his old foot missed them all, lost, looking for a point of reference and finding only gravel.

El Ferrocarril possessed a beautiful dehors of limestone arches, resembling an Andalusian-style café. What did he know about Andalusia? Had they called it that, some aficionado of Spain, to tie it to the presence of the tracks? But now the railroad no longer ran.

He pushed the gate of an establishment, looked for the sink, and let it run a little, before drinking from it. He refilled the bottle. "It's probably full of chlorine," he said to the lady who was waiting with her grandson to wash his feet. He went back to taking a few sips, and to make the lady laugh, he added, "They say a little bit takes the hunger away."

From the café, along with the music, came the smell of focaccias and pizzas. A stray dog roamed among the tables. He had never had a small dog. He called him over.

He knows you're like him, some things you can just smell. From time to time, perhaps because vagabonds often had a small dog accompany them, he had been asked, "You don't have a dog?"

He used to respond with a verse stolen from some book to see what effect it had on people.

"I, good people, am my own dog."

A smart ass, he liked to shock people, say things at the beach and then be sure they were thinking about it. He liked to shock people and at the same time, disliked being laughed at.

He took out some change and bought a piece of oily focaccia. He pulled a piece off the crust and gave it to the dog, but it was a satiate dog.

Beyond the tunnel, he warmed himself under the sun. Ruins of towers emerged from the sea, and halfway up the coast rose a tier of greenhouses and villas. Higher up, the highway sliced through the mountain. He imagined there were rich aquifers because seepage from the tunnel had forced him to skim the wall and jump over puddles.

Raising his eyes up at the ridges was his exercise, and in the summer, before dinner, he loved to stand before the sun in front of the parched cliffs and crevices which, by now, sat in the shadows.

From the side of Port Maurizio, which remained behind the hill of San Lorenzo, he could no longer see anything, but the sun shivered. He thought of all the times when going eastward, the opacity told by his creator had surprised him, and then, in order to understand his words and arcs, he had thought of the colors and valleys he saw now, at San Lorenzo, and in a little while, the one at Riva, Santo Stefano.

Anguish as he had felt it in Cervo. What else had they done to him this time?

Beyond the flooded, fence-enclosed tunnel, whose net he would have had to bend to exit, after a few dozen meters, there was no more gravel, no more, and in its place, he found a stupid asphalt road, often frequented by walkers and cyclists. The brown asphalt, with lines harshly separating the two-way path, allowed bicycles to circulate in the middle. There were planters, benches, and a railing which prevented people from jumping into the sea. Every hundred steps, a staircase descended to the rocks and another went back up to the Via Aurelia.

A church bell was ringing somewhere, and in the midst of so much amazement, the memory of the *Hail Mary* brushed him. He was a child, still in Sanremo, and the *Hail Mary* of Our Lady of the Coast would gather the farmers. He and Gino would see them pause, gathering tools and tying weights onto the mules' backs. They would wait for them by the wash house; the beasts would drink and walk a stretch of the plain in single file as if they were on a railroad, then descend to the valley.

He laid his backpack down, forearms on the railing, and looked ahead, as if to see Corsica and understand something.

A middle-aged man joined him and pulled lightly on the railing.

"Can we trust it?" the old man asked him.

"When we leave, it will still be here," the man assured him. Shaking it a bit to make sure it was solid, the iron structure, pink from the salty air, had vibrated dangerously.

He could have asked this man, no questions asked, with any comment about the actuality of that substitution, or the failure of Corsica, although it was still too early to say whether it would pop up tonight. And the usual salty things that to one seem to say who knows what, when the golden sludge sinks and the weight sometimes expels the cork island. He leaned back slightly from the railing and hinted a smile at the base of the rocks where a seabed of marine salad stirred.

The reflection of light off the crevices and the eroded minerals and all that perhaps made that coast look like any other coast—cliffs, rocks, agaves, seaweed—no, he thought, it wasn't a matter of asphalt instead of gravel, it was just that he had reached the place where he was from. That's all.

His hands within a meter of the stranger's, he let go first, his backpack slung over his shoulder, and walked slowly, the small steps of a child. His left hand dragged smoothly along the bar, feeling its lumps of rust and the oily coating left by the salty air. A wooden fence, like those found in a backyard, followed the iron, which he accompanied its rounded surface in the same way, ready to withdraw his hand where the beams promised a splinter.

No, in reality, he knew well how things were. The railroad was moved toward the mountains; surely, the news had been circulating for some time in the waiting rooms and among the maintenance crews. But he had never given these things any importance; until recently, the west was as far away as he had ever been in his life. If he tried to picture Sanremo, he could not even imagine it as a place, but rather a season.

There were strong smells–holm oaks, wisteria–and the air without passing trains was clean, contaminated only by the sea. Without the gravel, the last image of railroads was missing, and he could take deep breaths of the vegetation around him, and feel that he could do so in exactly the way that the lack of tracks and gravel detracted the landscape of any ferrous remnants of railroads.

An old, elegant couple–she with hiking poles–came toward him. He told them the most banal thing they could hear: he felt nostalgia for the railroad. He adjusted his shirt collar and, his hands behind his back, tilted his head to one side.

The man and the woman laughed. "You're better off now," said the woman.

Some of Berrino's seascapes, which he saw in Alassio, and the words of a novel, crossed his mind. The grazing light. The writer from a town further west, one who seemed to owe much to Calvino, used them. His lichenous and mangled heart flew over the olive trees...that was all he remembered; sometimes in libraries, he read with a kind of drowsiness that when he left, he remembered nothing.

"His lichenous and mangled heart...."

They knew him.

"We went to his house in San Biagio," the woman said.

"Ah, how I would love to go there."

"It's not at the ends of the earth, where are you from?"

"From a season...I was away a long time and I missed a few things. For example, I knew that instead of tracks, bikes passed through there, but deep down, I never fully believed it. That's it, I just didn't believe it."

He looked up at the greenhouses. Stakes, he said, all the way to the Albenga plain. He planted them well, all in a neat row, and tied the garden twine–he respected geometry–furrow after furrow.

One day, toward the end of Liguria, he had read in the newspapers that the writer's lichenous, mangled heart had also flown over the olive trees.

When he watched the sea, it was as if he were waiting for a train, but what was he returning to, to the words in books to be surprised to remember, to those who had forgotten him in the draft of a fable and laughed at him? It was always that drawing of conclusions and ending days with, "It doesn't matter". An aesthetic, the perfection of the stakes in a row. It doesn't matter. To have known a long time that they had set a trap for him, a stupid bike lane instead of tracks. It doesn't matter so he pretends to discover it now. And wonder what, then, about life?

A few ladies appeared to the east, announced by the pattering of hiking poles, and sat at the kiosk tables on the side of the sea, where he had sat and watched the salt-white prairie. An expanse of diamonds clustered in a narrow corridor before melting into purple, for a moment the glow faded. Something was expected from the waters, the miracle, the evaporation. And he, now that evening eroded the raw patina of colors, gave that miracle his back.

Even the ladies seemed to pay more attention to the air among the viburnums and gorse than to the work of the plow on the sea. The collapses and porous rolls in the geography repeated and nullified with each shudder, absorbed the secrets of reflections, and from the saline whiteness a vapor came off, rose, and reached beyond Sanremo, to the border. The azurite of the churches where he had knelt and all that burned was saved only in the ashes.

One of the ladies answered him, "Yes, it's nice here." The other, seeing him armed with a backpack, straps, and a cap, asked where he was coming from.

He motioned upward with his chin, toward that kind of future that has long passed, behind him.

He had ordered a cappuccino without foam and drank it, stopping only when the spoon could no longer scoop anything. He wiped his mouth before speaking.

"Imagine that a hundred years ago, those who gave their vegetable garden, because of expropriation, I suppose, for the construction of the railroad, asked for a document of intended use, in the sense that they said gentlemen, I will give you the vegetable garden but you can only build a railroad, and if one day, you remove the tracks and build a kiosk, the vegetable garden goes back to being mine, or my heirs'. Let's pretend that they signed such a document...after all, they knew very well that if they built a railroad there, it was for eternity...."

The ladies listened, amused, and looked at each other as if wondering whose turn it was to respond. The railroad went toward the mountains because they had been able to add more tracks that way. They had abolished some stations; theirs, for example, had been moved toward the mountains, and it was a horrible station. They were both from Castellaro and they were cousins.

"Does the railroad go through Castellaro?"

"No, but the one in Taggia is sort of ours, too...what about you?"

"I'm from Sanremo, from Bresca Square."

He remembered a girl, he still remembered her after such a long time. They were at the station in Arma and as she waited for the train, she had shared a focaccia with him. The saltwater melted nothing, leaking chloride and iodine, the steam furrowed etchings of a mythological Liguria.

"Where are you going?"

"Where the tracks end."

"Where are you going, dummy?"

"I don't know exactly."

"Go home, your mother must be looking for you...are you hungry? What school do you go to?"

He ate the cookie the waiter had served him with his cappuccino, digesting it.

"I get full right away, I used to eat a whole chicken," he said.

How old she must have been if she was still alive, considering she was at least four years his senior.

"If everything coincided, I should meet a very old lady around here. It would make sense, there is a logic that cannot be opposed."

The ladies did not smile.

"Have you ever seen the ocellated lizard?"

"Never, but they say it exists. People have seen it in Pompeiana. You?"

"Never seen it either."

The evening tremors played with the most unusual noises, spoons and ceramics. Typically his meals matched different noises: plastic, trays, containers in general, aluminum plates to be thrown away. "You know, I confess I've walked all my life along the tracks to see where they ended, but considering that they had died behind me, I could have come back sooner…or never left. Do you agree?"

"Have you worked?"

He liked they had switched to *tu*[9]. "Sure, I've hoed, planted stakes, watered, painted, been a watchman at a campground, and many years ago, I helped a lifeguard open beach umbrellas in the evenings and early mornings."

The ash had eventually made the mountains in the west resemble those in Tuscany. Although he had not had much time to get an impression of Tuscany. He told them how one decided on that lifestyle.

"What lifestyle?"

"The railroad vagabond lifestyle, I thought we had understood each other…." He had pulled an empty chair close to him to rest his arm on it. "It's just that we can't save anything."

"Sometimes dreams are enough," said the most talkative one, to follow that vein between the romantic but complicated path. She actually looked at that arm on the chair as if this man had put it on her shoulder.

"Come on, it's already a lot if one puts aside memories, ma'am."

He had already made peace with the fact that the tracks had died behind him a lifetime ago. As for dreams, they should never be realized, he thought, otherwise one loses them.

"Do you think it's mandatory to have a dream?"

The ladies did not comment.

---

[9] In Italian, *tu* is the informal way of addressing a person as "you." It is used between two people with a friendly and/or equal relationship, such as friends and family.

TOWARD BUSSANA

Evening had sprinkled light over the Via Aurelia, and a less bright dust rose from the greenhouses halfway up the coast.

He balanced his backpack from one shoulder to the other, but then he put on his jacket and the luggage weighed less. Entering the city and losing contact with the beaches, all hidden as they were by buildings, he found himself in the vicinity of the old Arma di Taggia station. The bike lane replaced every other railroad track, and this time, even the usual bunch of tracks was missing; only the ruins of the old building, secured and full of fences and panels, remained.

He put down his luggage and put his hands in his pockets. He looked between the panels, his lips barely parted. Then he returned to the bike lane, and began to feel, as he did every evening, the callus caused by the buckle of his backpack on his shoulder.

The bike lane divided the city. At that hour, most people were out to drink rather than bike. He didn't like it and decided to go down to the sea. But it was full down there too, ice cream parlors and cafés one after another, palm trees all the way to the sand.

Atop a ridge on the beach at Bussana, there were benches, and he put down his luggage. Lights beyond an abandoned building illuminated the Via Aurelia all the way up the hill, from which the church embedded with yellow and green lights overlooked, pine needles crossed other illuminations.

A few meters from the sea, he found a second little church, little more than a cave. It was closed, but from outside, through a grating, he could see the walls and ceiling made of a mixture of gravel and stone, the pews lit by candles. He drew his eyes closer to the grating and slowly made the sign of the cross, his forehead grazed by his fingertips, his chest, his shoulders one after the other, and his lips, on which his fingers lingered. At the base of the canvas of the Crucifixion of Jesus, a tea light glowed a palm away from the gorse vase.

Along the beach there was no shortage of shaded corners near the bathing establishments where he could lie down. He had bathed in that water, he had come here with Gino, and his mother had had to accompany them because neither of them knew how to swim yet. Had they walked here, from Sanremo? Maybe they had taken the bus; he noticed that it stopped on the Via Aurelia, just below the big church.

Nothing was true, the fact was that it had always seemed to him an obligation to remember the things of his childhood, a desire to profane the temple. Forced to invent memories and dynamics, places, days, notice a cliff quilted with agaves with fleshy, etched leaves, floating filth, sea foam, hear the swish of water, and smell sunscreen, so many were the deprivations of his former life that he had not been able to live, the beautiful frame around the blank canvas. No, he had never been to that place, not even in that water, only his mother had been able to tell him about it, telling him the story of the little church halfway up the coast, above the Via Aurelia. That was it, that little church was the real planet of his childhood.

He paused on the beach to look up again at the church, even though not even in there did he remember ever having been. Remembering as one remembers places that somehow belong to us like few others in the world even if we are seeing them for the first time. His life invented and already lived, his life used by others.

He descended the steps, reached the shore, and pulled the bottle and a leftover crust of bread out of his backpack. There was also fruit in a container he had bought in Arma. He liked fruit salad and he was tempted to eat it, but he held back. He lay down in front of the sea and searched for a taste of focaccia in that bread crust.

"Where are you going?"

"To see where the tracks end."

"Where are you going, dummy?"

"I don't know."

"Come on dude, go home, your mother must be looking for you...."

He did not let her say anything else.

From the road stretched a campsite and a cantilever slab; he combed through the area until he was under the slab, walking crouched down. Once he lay down, he was comfortable. He arranged his things on the gravel, his jacket next to him, and lay down on one side so he could monitor the church halfway up the hillside.

As he was about to fall asleep, he heard footsteps along the shore. Had it not been night, he would have been able to see their heads, and if they approached—they could have been boys—he would have noticed them from the waist down. If he did not move, they could not notice him. He was used to these situations, the watchful waiting in stations or escarpments, on beaches. The best part was when the moaning would start, and not only would they not let him sleep, but they would force him into immobility because on jumping out at that point, he would have to justify himself. Once a man had kicked and punched him. The woman eventually spit on him. Other times it had gone better, he had explained to himself. No, he was not a voyeur or anything like that, never, ever had he had that interest; he was just there to sleep. No, he was not there because he knew people were fornicating there; on the contrary, had he known, he would have chosen another place...but a vagabond is always wrong.

He awoke in the night from the cold and the need to empty his bladder. The night visitors were gone, the surf and sand smelled of seaweed and urine. It was almost dawn, and just before, the garbage men had stopped to take the dumpsters and the smell of garbage had replaced that of the beach.

The birds' turn. There must have been palm trees or some other trees around there. A hum of traffic came from under the Via Aurelia, more continuous and sustained than in the night.

The establishment's café was opening then. A good smell of croissants tortured him and he remembered the fruit container.

He pushed the luggage and came out from under there, taking to the shore. There came the faint roar of an already tired sea. His boots on the gravel made more noise. He took them off, his socks too, rolled his pants up to his knees, and penetrated the water up to his calves. The right pant leg lowered back down and the hem lapped at the water. He bent down to wash his feet, between his toes, then his hands, his face, and he began to feel hot. He undressed and folded his shirt, laying it on the gravel, his pants neatly spread out on a rock for the hem to dry, and remained in his underwear. He heard people talking from the terrace of the café; he laughed it off and ignored them. He went in only up to his thighs, rising on the tip of his toes when the peak of the wave threatened his underwear.

Below the Via Aurelia, halfway up the coast, the clear façade, the rose window, and the black edge of the pines, invaded by the daylight, could be seen clearly. At other times, were it not that he was coming back, he would have gone up, to wait for them to open and kneel.

Who knows why they chose up there, was there a reason why his father and mother had decided to get married in that church and not in Sanremo?

The city was surely awaiting him somewhere behind the cliff. He had put his shirt back on and was going barefoot, railroad hiking boots in one hand and luggage in the other, like a suitcase, so as not to hurt the calloused groove since the morning. He looked like a foreigner but was a native.

He would have liked to have had his photograph taken that day (no one but the island sketcher, whom there was never a chance of seeing again, had ever taken a photograph of him), his pants raised to his knees as he seemed to remember the farmers in the vegetable gardens above Sanremo wearing them, when they entered the small irrigation canals barefoot to tread the earth and remedy the collapses caused by moles; his sweat-colored cap, his shirt knotted at the bottom, and those dry calves. Backpack slung over his shoulder again, he walked half-happily, returning the beachgoers a smile, and with long strides, as if suddenly he felt he was running a bit late.

Before rounding the cliff and finally losing sight of the Bussana church, he looked up at it for a single moment. The novelists in the libraries called it melancholy, but in the stations and winter shelters of the beaches, in the underpasses, it had no name. And it had nothing to do with nostalgia, as some claimed. In his case, then, nostalgia for what? He had arrived. For a period of time maybe, he had read that one could be nostalgic even for a period of time. He had never been able to feel it, rather one could cultivate a nostalgia for the impossible, for a desire: the end of the tracks. He would have asked them, "Italo Calvino and Carlo Levi," who had laughed at him, "can you tell me what nostalgia someone like me can have?" And now that he had finally discovered the inglorious end of the tracks, was one to search for the nostalgia of destiny? He blamed himself for something, though, and in the last few nights, he had thought of nothing else. In Cervo, coming down from the Corallini Square and no longer seeing the tracks, he realized he made a mistake. He had to turn back around, enter the tunnel toward the east, and go toward its entrance because he had entered the tunnel, without going all the way through it. It was there, toward the east, over a fence, that sooner or later, the tracks ended.

Sanremo

On the Via Aurelia, he suddenly notices how much the city has grown, and he notices that it is her, beyond her dimensions, it is Sanremo. The city with the sidewalk with orange trees and palm trees, the traffic lights that once were not there, and the things that are now there, not as if they were waiting for him, but because they are part of a life able to exist in spite of him, to do so as they have always done, without him...is it possible that no one will notice?

Hey there, good, bored people, don't act indifferent, it's me.

They would have taken him for a crazy person.

And here is a nice store with the fruit stands set up outside, the awning for the sun, the tobacco shops, with the vertical sign like the ones he saw in Ligurian cities. And the monumental entrance to the stadium, inaugurated when he was a child; they even preserved the plaster that was the color of milky coffee. He played soccer in the alley with Gino then, and every afternoon, the bite of the humidity changed their movements, their precarious control of the ball, a beauty lost downhill every time.

The sea on the left and all those old buildings, the asthmatic trees, the crossroads, further past the square.... There's a special place he's been thinking about for almost a century, which he knows well where to locate, despite the fact that he could only see it in photographs in the library; it's high above, in line with Our Lady of the Coast. Villa Meridiana, that's where he needs to get to—is there a gate now, a fence protecting it from defilers? It doesn't matter, but is that the first place where he must go, to tell him I have arrived in the end, you see?

Why is he stalling? It must be because Bresca Square is much closer, that's it. There's Colombo Square, and Bresca Square is back there, and he's tired.

A pine tree, an ice cream parlor, a window display of books. The church and strips of colorful advertisement posters on each building's facade.

And so, this old man who had put his boots back on and left his pants rolled up at the knee, almost without realizing, goes straight to where he knows.

Bresca Square. He crosses it as if the long race of almost a century could not stop him, stumbling, tired and weak. He sets down his backpack.

But what exhaustion, on a day like today? He takes the last sip from the bottle and fills it at an iron fountain, near a puddle full of pine needles. He goes back to drinking. He leans over the railing and just about finds the spot again, were it not for that stupid brown asphalt bike lane in place of the tracks that ruins everything...there he is looking down and counting the bounces. The harbor will still be there, as well as Santa Tecla, further down, with its prisoners and old fortress cannons facing the city and not the sea.

He would gladly sit somewhere–he doesn't feel well–but the benches are all taken, and the former steps on which old men threatened to puncture the ball have become entrances to major restaurants and fish markets.

An elderly couple sits on the first bench with two small dogs on leashes, one calm, the other pulling to either side. The dog pulls and the elderly do not get up. On the second one, a mother and two children, one in a wheelchair, the other sitting on the ground collecting pine needles with his hands; the mother says nothing to him. On the third bench, two lovers, cell phones in hand; there might be some space on the corner of the bench. On the last one, an elegant, young lady, sitting on the end; he could sit next to her, but elegant women have never loved the idea of sharing a bench with him.

The young woman's bench is the one closest to the harbor as the crow flies. Something draws the old man's attention: the woman has stood up and is waving to someone in his direction. Because she continues, the old man turns to see who she is addressing, but there is no one behind him. He just can't see well from that far. The woman has resumed making polite gestures, and after a while, it's all clear to him: she is greeting him and signaling for him to join her, as if she had the authority. He picks up his luggage and obeys, passing the benches with the elderly with the little dogs, the lovers, the mother with the children. That's Bresca Square; the old man stops at an appropriate distance, tilts his head, gets a better look, and the young woman smiles at him. His lips part as he walks up to her.

"Mom." He repeats.

"Where have you been? I've been waiting for you for a long time."

And did you look for me? She knows what he is thinking and tells him, "Of course I thought of you and looked for you always. I never gave up. But why did you roll your pants up to your knee."

He puts his luggage down. He says, "Because, there is no reason," and pulls them back down. He goes over to hug her, and she lets him hug her. Many, many years ago she would have been much taller than him, and maybe until a few years ago, he would have been much taller, but now they are almost the same height. He feels that she does not put as much strength into her embrace as he does, or as much strength as she used to put into hugging him. Nevertheless, they hug each other for a long time. Her smile, on the other hand, is the same. He recognizes her smell and the violet scent she used to wear, but it is her unique smell that makes him think that even without recognizing the shape of her face, her eyes, and the warmth of her hands, and even without being able to see her, in the deepest darkness of a tunnel, even without her voice, he would recognize her by her mother's smell. Now he thinks he knows just what nostalgia is. It's not nostalgia for the past, or future, or a region, it's just nostalgia for ourselves.

"Did you wait for me that long?"

"Why do you ask?"

"Because. What about Gino? What about Dad?"

"They've been waiting so long for you, too–don't wipe your nose with your sleeve."

The old man nods and sits down.

"Are you tired?"

"Am I tired, Mom."

"Let's go home now. Are you hungry?"

"No, I'm not hungry."

But she sits down too, and together they look past the bike lane, at the top of the sea, which is perhaps no longer the sea, its outline between the rooftops and within the foliage of the pine trees. He didn't remember those pine trees in the middle of the square being that tall.

He would kick from one spot, more or less in line with the bench where the elderly couple with the little dogs sit–at one time, there weren't even benches–and the goal was where they sell fish now. Those who scored didn't become goalie; they did after playing a while, even if they always scored.

"I saw the little church in Bussana."

"How do you remember?"

"That you told me you got married in the church in Bussana? I remembered it when I saw it. Why didn't you get married in Sanremo?"

"Because."

She waits for him to ask her something. She expects many questions, one after another, but he also waits for her.

She tells him, "You are missing three teeth."

"I'm missing a lot of teeth...."

She seems to think about it, a little disappointed. She gets up. "Shall we go?"

Then he also stands up.

"Do you want me to carry the bag for you?"

"Yes, thank you," he tells her. "But just for a bit."

They smile at each other, hardly speaking. How strange, even their eyes rarely meet. Back in Sanremo, his eyes look up at things or stare at the asphalt covered with pine needles. Every now and then, he stops for a moment and turns to look at the corner of the square, his thumb and forefinger wiping the corners of his mouth, his tongue running over his lip.

She smiles. She must think that children sometimes make the gestures of older people, but there are things that only older people do.

He, too, resumes smiling. He doesn't know what else to do. "You are still very young." It must be strange for him to see her again this young, to see her anyway; how strange it must be for her to see him this old, to see him anyway. He no longer has the courage to call this woman mom, as he did just a little while ago, this woman, who has probably not been to the Bagni Paradiso to sunbathe in so long and is so pale, in the middle of summer, wearing a light, floral robe–not discolored, just out of style.

At a certain point, instead of going up the steps that leads to their porch, she invites him to go on, and he, calling her mama again, asks, "Aren't we going home, mom?"

"No, let's not go there."

He doesn't protest. He follows her, now carrying his own back-pack, but on the side where she isn't next to him, something he has never done in his life, carrying a bag with his other hand so he doesn't feel someone far away.

"You are so young."

"Don't mention it."

She watches him walk by her side, his suffering gait, on the verge of collapsing on the gravel with each step. In a window, they look at themselves standing side by side to see if they are the landscape.

Once at the old station, he wants to know something that is press-ing him, "Are we going to the Bagni Paradiso?"

"How did you figure it out?"

"I just did. There was a smell in the changing rooms; Mr. La Boz-zetta used to always give us number 12. They used to make *sardenaira*."

"The best in town."

On the promenade, seagulls fly over the palm trees. After being in silence for a while, he feels the desire to talk to her about the things he read in the libraries, watching the seagulls fly in the rain. The dusty olive terraces he saw shimmer in the evening and at dawn, the air absorbing the sea, and the olive terraces under which he immersed himself, living in the tunnels, and catching their juices. But he fears that words will drag away the enchantment, desecrate it. And he is no longer anyone's literary invention.

Following the movement of the palm trees, as he followed that of the tufts of reeds, in the places farthest from the world, where no one lives nor dreams. His unknown and secret railroad region, he, seen by the world only fleetingly through a train window. Who might this man have been? Was he really there? Did you see him? The child, the boy, the young man, the man, the old man, sitting on the ground on the gravel with his hands holding his folded legs, as a child holds them.... He fears that telling her all this will move the words side by side in a long, silent line; this he fears, that somehow she will also shift an inti-mate center of gravity and address him with words related to the writer from Sanremo, from when, maybe right after the war, Calvino would sit on the benches with that lawyer.

"So many mutilated palm trees, right?" he tells her.

"I can't get used to it...they all used to be the villas of rich but also sad people, they used to come here and to Bordighera, Ospedaletti...now, fortunately, for certain diseases there are remedies."

"What did Dad do for a living?"

"He worked at the casino in Ospedaletti. He played music, he liked jazz...do you like jazz? You used to listen to it as a child."

"Jazz not so much, I like simple music, accordions...and then he left the casino?"

"Then Ospedaletti closed it down."

"And where did he go?"

"To play elsewhere, in small orchestras. He played with Freddy, a friend of his."

"And then what?"

"Then, a long, long time later, you were born, then you were born."

He nods. What can he ask her? "If I were still a child, what would I do?"

"What questions are you asking me? You would ask me so many questions, yes, like now."

"Did I really ask that many questions?"

"It's normal, you were a normal child...and one time, you came home and said you almost found out what you wanted to be when you grew up, only your little friend Gino had already said it...."

"And what was it?"

"Don't you remember?"

"Yes, well."

Pasquali's Statue of the Primavera is white, slender like her, and wears the same ancient, colorless robe.

"Up there, there were olive trees, and over there, beyond our Lady of the Coast, that writer's father used to cultivate...." She looked at him as if to say, "If you don't want to, we won't talk about it."

Then she asked him one thing. "How did you survive in the tunnels? There must be nothing more dangerous."

"If there was no sidewalk next to the gravel, I wouldn't go in. Not even if the tunnel was from here to there."

"What if the sidewalk narrowed or ended halfway through?"

"I would turn around, exit and go up at around 5 in the afternoon, which means I would take the long way around the edge of the cliff."

They had resumed walking, and he switched the luggage to his other hand. In front of a café or bakery, they saw a tall, elegant gentleman, his hair as white as the statue, newspapers in his hand, and his mother returned him a half bow as one greets great poets.

"Gino," said the old man, after putting down his backpack for a moment. "To be salt water, he wanted to be water so he was the sea."

"So he was the sea."

"The seawater is not as salty as it used to be."

Past the café-bakery, they went down the narrow staircase a few steps, her ahead, then at the bottom they found the bike lane and walked side by side again.

They could see the waves, their white crests, perfectly distant from each other and between them, the purple of the sea, but neither of them wished to stop and look.

He recognized a gate; he had not thought of that place in a lifetime, yet he had walked past it many times as a child. Now it was clear to him again. His mother said what it was called, perhaps because even for her, he thought, the places that were not mentioned did not belong in any atlas.

He was tired and the backpack was as heavy as if he were dragging a crossbar.

His mother offered him her hand, and he put the weight back into the other. He no longer knew how to carry that backpack, and for the first time during his railroad life, he wished he had left it somewhere, hung his cap and backpack on the cemetery gate, and pretended to forget them.

She said, somewhat disappointed, as if she had discovered more missing teeth, "How could you forget some things?"

"Do you mean the name of the Monumental Cemetery?"

She nodded, "And to do the sign of the cross, I mean...let us recite an *Eternal Rest*."

Rocked by the undertow, Englishmen, Russians, and Jews rested in all those graves, and they had been there for so long that the tangle of stones crumbled by the sun and salt, welded together by ivy and other flowering vines, would be said to be dwellings inhabited by a civilization gone to ruin.

As a child, he had therefore walked by without paying attention to that cemetery, and after so many years, he, too, tried to think about with it. One tried to think about it, sooner or later, he thought. And it was as if the old bones, the dust, and the flowering vines, and what brushed against, wrapped around, and crowded all that foreign death that died in Sanremo, somehow embraced each other underground until they were one waiting being.

He put his veiny hand on the bar, more out of a desire to squeeze something and hold on than to push the gate.

His old, uncertain voice followed the young one with a slight delay, for he did not remember the *Eternal Rest* well and went on repeating the words after her, who knew them perfectly. They recited three of them. Had it been the *Hail Mary*, he would have recited it by heart too, for he recited it almost every night of his life. But he never said the *Eternal Rest* before falling asleep.

She reached for his hand and he removed it from the iron roughness, where he had laid it again after making the sign of the cross, and held it out to her. For the first time, her hand felt a bit fat and warm, a firmer texture and grip, whereas until now it had seemed to him the grip of a distracted hand.

Once more he became conscious of something that lowered his eyelids again because a mother's smell had wafted strongly through the air.

"At one point, I thought about how old you were. I thought about it...."

"That I was dead?"

"I was old myself."

"And you felt a sense of guilt for not being at my funeral...if you knew mine, I would exchange yours for my guilt. And you couldn't have known...it's like for me, it's not like I could have known where you were...were you going forward, backward? Who knows what paths you had taken, life is full of twists and turns."

He did not reply and she went on, searching for words. "I used to ask everybody and they would say yes, someone like that was here...but time passed and I lost you, you transformed, I mean you grew, you became you...you have so much of your father...."

He pulled the rusty old bolt out of his backpack, made the gesture of someone showing off a toy, and with the gentleness with which one lays a crystal glass on the table, placed it between them, in the center of the bench where they had sat to rest, beyond the cemetery.

"I was still a boy when I found it...I used to put it on drawings so that the wind wouldn't carry them away."

"Was it that windy?"

"It's a railroad wind, Mom, always rolling, one way or the other and bringing dust, leaves...how many leaves fly on the tracks, you'd say a train would have to stop against it, that's why they have maintenance crews...the wheat kernels from the cars, the litter...when I was a boy, I used to walk playing a game: my foot had to go from crosstie to crosstie. One day, I broke my foot, not far away, past Riva Ligure...."

The volume of mountains at the border and the edge of graves blackened in the air, his vision blurred. In one corner–he could be mistaken–it seemed to him that carob trees and tufts of reeds were growing. He remembered when he used to play with Gino in Bresca Square and then run home all sweaty, and before bathing him, she would take him to the terrace and show him where the sun fell. Not where it died, the sun could not die, as it could not be born, she had taught him. He would wake up like a spider and, after going through the web and checking that everything was holding up, he would stumble upon something and hide on the ground a few hours. A pretense, he would play dead so as not to be killed by the moon and then, when she got distracted and could no longer burn him, he would get back up.

Now he wouldn't have wanted to remember this kind of light-hearted thing, the myth of childhood didn't count, those who talked about it in books in Ligurian libraries claimed that the myth came later, while back then it was just the reality of a child, freshly bathed, a terrace, the sun at the end...no, he didn't want to, fearing that if he squinted and remembered the memories set aside, she, too, would disappear from that evening without warning, like the moon.

He would have liked to eat something, yes, he felt the need and specifically had a great craving for fruit. Maybe it was his thirst, his dry throat, like in the tunnels after a freight train had passed.

Beyond the bench, under that stupid bike lane, there was a long rectangle of land between the establishments. In one corner of the vegetable garden, a farmer was working, despite the hour; in fact, along the bike lane the streetlights had already turned on, and the farmer was picking up his tools. He had filled the basket with vegetables and was about to leave.

His mother stood up and looked both ways before crossing the bike lane. She asked the man if he could give her a watermelon, one of the nice ripe ones lying on the ground.

The farmer scratched his head. "A couple of pears, ma'am?"

"No, the child really wants a watermelon. You have so many."

The farmer looked up again at the edge of the bike lane and at the knees of the woman praising his watermelons, and went back to scratching his head under his hat. She looked around, felt the pockets of her floral robe, but had nothing. Finally, she slipped off her wedding ring.

"Here, the best watermelon, I beg you."

"Ma'am, are you crazy? I will give you the watermelon, just come back tomorrow and give me a couple of euros…a gold wedding ring for a watermelon, I mean are you crazy?" he repeated.

"Keep the wedding ring, good man, we just want the watermelon, you know…." Since the farmer would not accept the exchange, she threw the ring into the soil under the light of the street lamp because she wanted the watermelon at all costs. The farmer shook his head, bent down to pick up the ring, and chose the best watermelon.

It was a watermelon that was just ripe enough, he said, the kind ready to open as soon as the tip of the knife touched it. He rinsed it under the faucet. "Oh, but I don't put anything on it, all natural stuff," he assured her. He asked her if she wanted him to slice it for her, and she thought that was a very good idea.

He prepared it on a small table against the wall, under the light, where he kept scissors and string, irrigation fittings. He approached the wall by the bike lane and she bent down, holding her skirt as women do.

"Put one hand under it," said the farmer.

The woman thanked him, received the cardboard box with the entire watermelon sliced into slices, and holding it from underneath so that the weight would not break through the cardboard, crossed the bike lane (rarely did a bike pass by) and sat down next to her son.

There was light shining from floodlights among the eucalyptus trees of an establishment, and the old man only now noticed it. Beyond the cliff and the illuminated houses, there must have been other establishments and hotels, and further beyond was where the sun had sunk. From below a bright sign came catchy music.

To stay close together, she had not put the box between them, keeping it next to her on the end of the bench. When the old man asked for a slice, she handed it to him.

"Is it good?"

"It's a banana." They laughed a little. It was long ago, when she would peel an apple and give him slice after slice, but he wouldn't finish it, so she made him think it was a banana, saying, "Eat one more piece."

"We never went to the Bagni Paradiso again."

"No."

"Did we forget to?"

"Yes."

He asked her nothing else. Busy as he was and leaning forward so as not to soil his shirt, he ate greedily. Too greedily. The pulp, on passing between his missing teeth, made a whistling sound.

While she was bargaining for watermelon, it had occurred to him to ask her something, and he did so now, between slices.

"Was I really a normal child?"

"What questions do you ask, of course you were normal."

"Tell me, please. I need to know. I have asked myself many times and a lie would hurt me more."

She was silent for a moment and looked at the top of the bean plants in the garden, the color of the moon. Some were exactly at her eye level, others at street level, barely peeking out.

"Tell me."

"A person with those kinds of thoughts is quite normal, you were more than normal...you were you, you were free." She tilted her head, then straightened it and turned it back to him.

He wiped his nose with his sleeve and said to her, "I was asking because something always felt off...." And he laughed with his mouth half-opened. *About me anyway*, he meant. Who didn't feel off once life passed, but even before that, at any moment, who could live and not feel off?

She said something as if she had translated it from the dialect, and they laughed about it.

"You didn't have much to sell anyway...." Maybe she had learned the dialect, too, during all that time since he had left and she had been waiting for him, looking for him, even in the dialect.

"You know, Mom, someone talking about you, saying something is off about you, that you're an idiot...."

She put her finger to his lips, signaling him to be quiet. "Don't get angry now."

"You're right. It doesn't matter."

Once he quenched his thirst, he took to eating with less fury. He looked for the Opinel knife in his backpack pocket, wiped it on the sleeve of his pants, cut a piece of watermelon from the slice, and skewered it. He was ashamed that he had not done this sooner. He removed a couple of seeds and handed it to her. She shook her head, she didn't want any. She would have asked him if she wanted any, she didn't want any. She continued to watch him eat that little seedless piece and immediately cut another, and she wanted to tell him to eat slowly.

He wiped his mouth with the back of his hand, and at one point, pulled a T-shirt out of his backpack–he shrugged, as if to reproach himself for his intention to use a poorly folded T-shirt, and at the same time, to act like he gave a damn–and with one edge, he wiped his hands and mouth better.

The backpack occupied the remaining piece of the bench, teetering on the edge and ready to fall off at any moment. He could have put it on the ground next to the bench, but that side was dirty. She said, "Give it to me, I'll keep it here where it's clean."

"Let's not forget it though."

"No, but if you want, I can carry it after for you."

He thought about it and nodded, but pretending he didn't understand, he asked her, "You'll carry it for me first?"

She did not respond, and he asked her nothing more.

They were silent for a long time—perhaps the longest they had ever been—almost as if they now agreed on everything, and as if that darkness was sacred and one had to learn to welcome it as of now, in silence.

Only the issue of the Bagni Paradiso remained to be resolved, although it no longer seemed of great importance. Unless he attributed a different meaning to it.

"We never went swimming again because there's no more time?"

"Don't think about these things, I wanted you to eat the watermelon and the farmer was going to leave—are you done?"

"No, I'll have some more," he said decisively.

Then she handed him another slice, and then another, and he held the last one in his hand for a long time. He cut tiny pieces off it, and the watermelon slice slowly released its juice.

"You don't want any more?" she asked.

"I know we only have the time it takes to eat the watermelon, you know." *And I'd like to take it*, he thought.

"Don't cry," she said.

He said okay. "I won't cry. Neither will you."

"No, I won't cry, and besides, there's still watermelon," she said. "Do you want to rest your head on my shoulder?"

"Then I won't be able to eat the watermelon...but you're right, I can also eat it later...do you want to rest your head on my shoulder?"

"Yes, you know, I'm tired, but can you still eat if I rest my head?"

He said yes, and he also wanted to tell her that he was not scared for himself, but he would have been lying, for he was scared for her. So beautiful and young, his mama all his life, the long time of the watermelon begun in Sanremo, or rather, not far away, in Bussana, on her wedding day, when she was already waiting for the watermelon eater.

If he thought it was not right for that breeze to end like that, he was not afraid, but it was only because he had never thought about it so much. Although one couldn't even say that; he had always thought about it—he had never thought about anything else—only now he was afraid.

She looked at him and shook her head. He did not understand.

She rested her light head on his bony shoulder, hard like a track, and from then on, he sat still. He doubted whether it was the weight of her head on his shoulder, or the calloused groove left by his backpack, which burned his neck and weakened him. He did not move, however, because he was certain that she had fallen asleep. And only then did he realize that just before, before resting her head on his shoulder, she had looked at him long and hard and had shaken her head because she would never see him again. He closed his lips slightly.

He wanted to delay the end of the watermelon, but somehow by mutual agreement, they had finished it. When he had asked her how many more slices were left, she had said two, and he had accepted the little lie as if they had also agreed on claiming it was not the last slice. Then he had dried his hands again on the edge of his shirt.

Now, however, he wanted to get up again to pee (all that water, a whole watermelon). He wanted to toss the rinds and wash his hands; they felt as sticky as the times he lowered a fig branch and helped himself, on the hills above the tunnels. He resented his thirst; the watermelon had taken away only the tiniest bit.

He did not move. He remained like that for a long time, her light head on his shoulder and the Sanremo breeze, a small amount of distracted stars perpendicular to the islands, the moonlit corridor off the Bagni Paradiso.

In the morning, the runners saw him on the bench, old and alone, watermelon rinds beside him on the cardboard, and found him in the same place when they ran by again. Flies sought the rinds and settled on his timeless hands. When the sun rose over everything and a while had passed since the farmer had returned to the vegetable garden below the bike lane, they learned that the old man had been sitting on the bench since the night before; he must have been a poor man and before going home, the farmer had offered him half of a watermelon.

General information about the farmer was noted. A policeman was ordered to search a few dozen square meters around the bench. Next to the old man's fingers, on the edge of the polished and varnished wood, stood the ancient yet not very rusty object, considering it belonged to a living hand for so long, clasped between fingers and scraped on the tracks, by someone living inside a fable, under a cloak on rainy days.

The policeman took the bolt, inserting a pen through the hexagonal shape, and put it in a bag. Under another bench and in the groove of a culvert, where the other policeman had gone to patrol, there was some litter among the reeds and shrubs. He glanced at it, broke a twig, and poked all over the soft ground of vegetation and mud. Then he went back up. There was nothing there. Not even along the fence nor in the farmer's vegetable garden. "Nothing," he said from down there. He pulled up a few rags with the twig and moved a small bottle still smelling of beer, thrown last night by the revelers, a sheet of newspaper. He broke the strange membrane, green-blue and transparent...what was it? The abandoned skin of a large reptile, or cellophane, maybe even latex. "Nothing," he said.

"Come up," ordered the superior.

"He didn't say anything else to you?" he asked the farmer.

"What else was he supposed to say to me? He accepted the half watermelon and thanked me several times."

"Did he have any luggage?"

"At first, I thought so. He had a bag with him, one of those beach bags, but now I see it's gone...."

IJmuiden, August 2022

AUTHOR'S NOTE

Can it be said that by dint of recounting Liguria's verticality, one can end up disowning it or wishing to invent a counterbalance to it? In my case, I thought about and felt it as the need for a change, but it was something that came from afar, something to be attributed to the matter of Holland. Essentially, by dint of laying out prose at a flat altitude like the Dutch kind, one ends up getting too invested. Recounting a horizontal Liguria could have become a challenge then, but challenges have never excited me. The thing is, if you lose a challenge, you get upset, and if you win one, you're forced to look for another. A challenge is like a dream, and if you accomplish it, argues the child who grew up in these pages, you are left without one, which is not good, because at a certain point, you become so used to chasing the image of the dream, that without it, you find yourself off course, without direction.

Come to think of it, in the end, I don't really know how the idea of a horizontal Liguria came about. Maybe I started writing and after a while I discovered that, without realizing it, I was really recounting a Liguria different from my usual ones, and that Liguria was located a few meters above sea level. A novel as straight as the tracks and almost as long as Liguria, but such a thing is not a novel, it is a map, something purely geographical and at the same time chronological. Although these coordinates are often transgressed. One example: In the 1930s, when the boy is still a boy and swims under the Foce neighborhood in Sanremo, he will collect episodes of his life, and during his railroad *flânerie*, he will remember that bathing establishment as the Bagni Paradiso, but in all likelihood no beach in Sanremo was still called that. Another example, this time geographical: From Carlo Levi's villa, you may be able to see the railroad, while from these pages, I am sure you cannot. Little things like that. And another inaccuracy: Perhaps Duilio Cossu, one of Calvino's childhood friends, did not become a lawyer, but in these pages, it is claimed that he did. And there is no reason why. Just as there is no reason for Walter Benjamin to have sought out a certain animal. Benjamin had been to Sanremo three times, and it does not appear that he was ever interested in the ocellated lizard. Perhaps he did not even know it existed, just as it is likely that he never met Calvino as a boy, but in the first few pages of this story, things happened exactly as they are described and as if they were true, and perhaps they are. In the end, what I was interested in was the story of a lost ball, deflated by time, but after Alfred Polgar's *The Small Balloon*, I do not think it is possible to add anything more to the undoing of a ball. It seemed to me then that one possibility still remained: to begin a story exactly where Polgar's child protagonist cries over the loss of the ball and is scolded severely and escorted out of the room. There in that moment and in that "outside," begins this other child's journey.

I often spoke to Giuseppe Conte about this project, and I thank him for listening to me. And for reading my work. Duilio Cossu, who I claim to be a lawyer in the novel, and is a peer and friend of Italo Calvino (which he actually was), will recount the time spent and games played with Italo, Eugenio, and his high school friends in the interviews he will give (the interview belongs to a book by Romano Lupi, *La città visibile*, which is fundamental for me). And it will be he, Duilio Cossu, who will reveal Calvino's desire to recount the adventures of the child who played ball in the alleys of Sanremo. But Calvino, apart from talking about it with friends, never wrote this story. As for Lupi's book, I no longer owned it, perhaps I had never owned it, and one day Franca Anfossi gave it to me. So I thank her too, and I thank Dario Voltolini for a sentence he gifted me in front of the sea in Port Maurizio, on the Parasio rock, at the Santa Chiara Loggia. For the readings and some advice on the structure, I thank Graziella Belli, Marco Federici Solari, and finally, Roberto Moriani for the documents on the partisan Calvino. Lastly, the publishing house. I worked alongside a very good team, especially Alessandro Gazoia, who was able to make me understand that if the vine has too many leaves and too many clusters it is not good, but he, at that point, was also able to show me where to subtract.

ABOUT THE AUTHOR

Marino Magliani was born in 1960 in Dolcedo, Liguria, in the Imperia area. He was born in a hospital which is now a home for the elderly. When he was twenty, he left for South America: Chile, Uruguay and Argentina where he lived for a long time.

He currently lives in Ijmuiden, on the Dutch coast, a land of sand, with buildings built on sand and trees that grow on sand and where the wind erosion is very strong. A docker, he devotes his life to writing and translating. He translates from Spanish and collaborates with the Italian Institute of Culture for the Netherlands. His latest novels include *Aren'aria* (2016), *Il creolo e la costa* (2016), *L'esilio dei moscerini danzanti giapponesi* (2017), *Prima che te lo dicano altri* (2018), *Il cannocchiale del tenente Dumont* (2021), *Materiali onirici di un somarello marino* (2024), *Sporca faccenda, mezzala Morettini*, con Marco Ferrari (2024). Between short story collections, poetry books, and graphic novels, he has yet another dozen or so pubications.

Much of his work has appeared among finalists if not winners of prestigious literary competitions. His stories appeared in various magazines and journals including *Ombrone, Maltese narrazioni, Nuovi Argomenti* and *Nazione Indiana*. He writes for the travel magazine *Alibi per essere altrove* and edits *La Poesia e lo Spirito*.

ABOUT THE TRANSLATOR

Orianna Soublette was born in Louisville, Kentucky to Venezuelan parents. She currently lives in South Florida where she works as a translator, editor, and tutor of English, Spanish, and Italian. At Florida Atlantic University, she received degrees in Psychology and Italian Language, Literature, and Linguistics. She has translated works of fiction and poetry. To learn more about Orianna Soublette's work, visit oriannasoublette.com.

Voci Italiane

This book series is dedicated to those works directly related to Italy, which may have their origins in Italy or abroad. They may be prose, poetry, criticism, history, and the like.

Marino Magliani. *The Boy and The Islands (A Dream of Calvino's)*. Translated by Orianna Soublette. Volume 1. ISBN 978-1-955995-16-0

Casa Lago Press Editorial Group

David Aliano	Donatella Izzo
Leonardo Buonomo	John Kirby
William Boelhower	Chiara Mazzucchelli
Ryan Calabretta-Sajder	Emanuele Pettener
Nancy Carnevale	Mark Pietralunga
Stephen J. Cerulli	Joseph Sciorra
Donna Chirico	Ilaria Serra
Fred Gardaphé	Anthony Julian Tamburri
Paolo A. Giordano	Sabrina Vellucci
Nicolas Grosso	Leslie Wilson

www.ingramcontent.com/pod-product-compliance
Lightning Source LLC
Chambersburg PA
CBHW032052260626
47157CB00020B/3068